THE

Wedding Dress

CHRISTMAS

Endorsements for Rachel Hauck

THE WEDDING DRESS

"Hauck weaves an intricately beautiful story centering around a wedding dress passed down through the years. Taken at face value, the tale is superlative, but considering the spiritual message on the surface and between the lines, this novel is incredible. Readers will laugh, cry and treasure this book."

—RT Book Reviews, TOP PICK!

THE WEDDING CHAPEL

"Hauck tells another gorgeously rendered story. The raw, hidden emotions of Taylor and Jack are incredibly realistic and will resonate with readers. The way the entire tale comes together with the image of the chapel as holding the heartbeat of God is breathtaking and complements the romance of the story."

—RT Book Reviews, TOP PICK!

THE WEDDING SHOP

"*The Wedding Shop* is the kind of book I love, complete with flawed yet realistic characters, dual timelines that intersect unexpectedly, a touch of magic and a large dose of faith. Two breathtaking romances are the perfect bookends for this novel about love, forgiveness and following your dreams. And a stunning, antique wedding dress with a secret of its own. This more than just a good read—it's a book to be savored."

—Karen White, New York Times Bestselling Author

THE ROYAL WEDDING SERIES

"Rachel Hauck's inspiring *Royal Wedding Series* is one for which you should reserve space on your keeper shelf."

—USA TODAY

THE MEMORY HOUSE

"Accomplished Hauck demonstrates genre finesse as she blends inspirational romance with a cinematic style of storytelling, bringing empathic characters to life as they cope with grief in marriage and faithfulness, parenthood and adoption, death and tragedy. Challenging decisions, the blessing of finding love again, and the solace of a beautiful Victorian home all come together in this spellbinding, lovely novel."

—Booklist Review

THE FIFTH AVENUE STORY SOCIETY

"You are cordially invited, dear reader, to step through the doors of an enchanting old library and embark on a remarkable journey with the *Fifth Avenue Story Society*. In this beautifully written novel, Rachel Hauck has created a cast of masterful characters whose stories seem shattered beyond hope. But Rachel doesn't leave them in their brokenness. She sweeps up the pieces and begins sculpting together a new story. A better story for each of them. Their fireside society is a place where miracles still happen. A space full of wonder to savor and dream. If you dare to step inside these pages, into this mysterious story society, you'll be warmly welcomed as a fellow sojourner and friend."

—Melanie Dobson, bestselling author of
Catching the Wind and *Memories of Glass*

"Rachel Hauck's rich characterization and deft hand with plotting and setting had me enthralled until I turned the last page of this superb novel. *Fifth Avenue Story Society* is truly a masterpiece—a one-of-a-kind novel that lingers long after the last page is turned. This is one I'll reread often, and it should garner Hauck much well-deserved acclaim. This should be on everyone's shelf."

—Colleen Coble, USAToday bestselling author of
the Lavender Tides series and *Strands of Truth*

Also by Rachel Hauck

Visit www.rachelhauck.com

This Time (ebook only)
Hurricane Allie (novella ebook)
Georgia on Her Mind

NASHVILLE SERIES
Nashville Dreams
Nashville Sweetheart

LOWCOUNTRY SERIES
Sweet Caroline
Love Starts with Elle
Dining with Joy

SONGBIRD NOVELS WITH SARA EVANS
The Sweet By and By
Softly and Tenderly
Love Lifted Me

THE WEDDING COLLECTION
The Wedding Dress
The Wedding Chapel
The Wedding Shop

THE

Wedding Dress

CHRISTMAS

RACHEL HAUCK

To God from whom all blessings flow.

Chapter One

JOJO

In the glow of the town's newly strung Christmas lights, all her fears seemed to fade. How could anxious thoughts survive in the gold and silver of the most wonderful time of the year?

Yet JoJo's fears resided deep. They rattled in her bones. Born from adversity and rooted in experience. She'd hoped to escape the family "curse," but it followed her. All the way to Dallas and back again.

Even so, on this glorious, cold afternoon before Thanksgiving, she sensed change lurking in the gentle breeze. A kind of change wrapped with hope and joy.

Surely she imagined things. But change in her life, her family's, especially around Christmas, meant pain, betrayal, trauma, and death.

Yet there was no place like her beloved hometown. And Hearts Bend, Tennessee, as of this moment, was dressed for the holidays and beaming with a million lights.

"Okay, boss lady, what do you think?"

JoJo turned to Lem McLeroy, the town's utility manager, as he collapsed his ladder.

"Magical. You and your crew worked hard, Lem. Thank you. And I'm not your boss lady. Just the volunteer coordinator."

"Are you sure?" Lem said with a bit of a laugh and sass. "Seems like you did a lot of *bossing* while me and the boys hung the wreaths, strung lights, and dangled the garland."

"I prefer the word *visionary*."

Lem's deep chuckle shook his round belly. "I guess that's why they pay you the big bucks."

Her turn to laugh. "Yes, city planning volunteers are among the rich and famous."

"Just you wait, Jo. Your ship's coming in."

"My ship? In the middle of Tennessee? Now that *would* be a miracle."

"'Tis the season," he said, surveying the lamppost lights, their small glow lost in the last of the sunshine.

"Well, my season can just stay nice and calm. *Miracles* for me seem to come in the form of disaster." She avoided his expression by going over her checklist one more time. "My ship is a broken-down canoe with only one paddle and a hole in the bow."

"Shew-wee, girl, that's some positive thinking right there." Lem walked toward his truck, ladder in tow. "I feel inspired."

"I call 'em like I see 'em."

Or lived them. But since she'd returned home five years ago, the dark cloud seemed to have passed from the Castle family. And she was grateful.

So she gave back to her safe, cozy, charming hometown. She chaired the Spring Garden Planting Committee to improve the renovated and beautiful downtown. Coordinated the fundraiser for the new pavilion in the park. Used her public relations experience to spearhead the Bash the Trash campaign, which taught the younger generation the streets and parks were not the city dump. Painted sets and walls at the Kids Theater. Even directed the Christmas play last year and the one before.

She had no idea what she was doing but faked it well enough. People applauded at the end. Thank goodness Ami-Jean Pringal replaced her this year.

The best part about being back in Hearts Bend was being with her family. She worked with her cousin Haley Danner at The Wedding Shop. Not her original dream job of taking the public relations world by storm, but one she fell in love with more every day. The brides, the gowns, the whole wedding process charmed her.

And was probably the closest she'd ever get to being a bride. Romance had not gone well for her lately. If ever.

But she found solace and comfort tucked away in her old room, living with her parents and Uncle Ben, not missing her swanky Dallas loft with the swanky pool on the rooftop. Well, maybe sometimes. Until she remembered *that* night.

No, being home was best. Safe. With the shine off her wanderlust. Besides, Daddy and Mama needed her. Found comfort in her presence.

And, oh her sweet Daddy melted her heart the day she came home from a weekend of bridal shows with Haley to see he'd knocked a hole in her bedroom wall in order to annex the attic stairs.

"For your own sitting room," he said, clearing his throat beneath the soft tone of his voice.

Took him two years to finish, but JoJo had a private space. Not that she used it all that much.

What she loved most about home was being five years and six hundred miles from the nightmare. From that dreadful night.

Lem returned to where she stood staring toward the park, toward a fading yet real memory. "Jo, the boys and I are going to Ella's Diner for a late lunch. Care to join us? My treat." He approached her, squinting through a bright but thin ribbon of sunlight, zipping his jacket against the cold.

She glanced at her phone. It was going on four.

"Thanks but I need to get to the shop. We're decorating tonight for Black Friday. And Haley is making the pies for our family Thanksgiving dinner and hasn't even started. So she wants to finish early."

But it was usually midnight before they had the shop dazzling with Christmas lights and cheer.

"Black Friday and a wedding shop. Somehow my man brain never put those two things together." Lem scratched his head as if he really wanted to understand.

"You have a daughter who will probably get married one day, Lem. Trust me, she'll be wanting the best dress for the best price."

"She says she's going to wear her granny's, but by the looks of her closet, I'll be steering her and my wife to your Black Friday sale when the day comes."

"I hate to tell you, but she's already been in." JoJo started for the shop. "Charge your lunch to the city account."

But Lem's head was down, phone pressed to his ear. "Gracie, are they *that* serious?"

JoJo grinned at the snippet of conversation. Dads were always the last to know.

At the corner of Blossom and First Avenue, she paused as Old Man Exley slowly approached the stop sign in his '70s era Cadillac, looked both ways twice and then slowly turned the corner.

He gave JoJo a single horn blast and she waved as she crossed toward the shop, which sat regal and beautiful in the light of the setting sun, the large pane windows soaked with a golden glow.

The three-story structure with an apartment featuring gables and turrets was built in 1890 by Haley and JoJo's great-aunt Jane. Since then the shop had dressed almost seventy thousand brides in the last 130 years and she was proud to join the family tradition.

Whatever made her think she had to "see the world?" Everything she needed, everyone she loved, was right here in Hearts Bend. Including the Wedding Shop, her favorite place in town.

Especially at Christmas. She and Haley decorated a large tree, trimmed the windows with twinkle lights and set caroling statues in the small front lawn.

"Lovely evening isn't it, JoJo?"

She'd just made it to the other side of the street when a man wearing a brilliant purple shirt approached. His brown hair was in need of a comb but the spark in his blue eyes seemed to radiate all over his whole face.

"A bit cold, but yes, lovely." She stepped backwards toward the shop. Did she know this man?

Steady. You're fine. It's Hearts Bend. In the afternoon.

"We'll have a white Christmas," he said.

"You sound sure of yourself."

"Because I am." His gaze never left her face. Never blinked or faltered.

"I'd best be going. Work and all." She motioned toward the shop.

"Yes, I know." He started in the opposite direction. "Don't be afraid, Jo. Change is in the air, and it's good."

"Change? What change? And how do you know me?" She didn't like being known by a stranger.

"Have a good evening, JoJo."

She shivered as he tipped an imaginary hat and walked on, crossing the avenue toward the town center. For a flash second, a memory surfaced. She had seen him before. Yes, but the scene was dark and murky. Where was she? What was she doing? Then the moment faded before she could arrange the scattered pieces.

Hearts Bend boasted a population of 10,223. It was impossible to know everyone. But Jo was pretty sure she knew everyone who knew her. Ah, never mind. Probably an old friend of Daddy's.

And now she was really late. Depositing her decorating checklist in the passenger seat of her semi-faithful '83 Datsun 280ZX parked beside the shop on Blossom Street, JoJo made her way to the shop, entering through the back porch door.

When she first started working with Haley, she spent a lot of summer evenings here, talking, laughing, eating takeout from Ella's or The Fry Hut with Haley and her husband Cole.

Then they remodeled their house. After all, he did own his own construction company. When they finished their house, they took on her parents' kitchen upgrade project. And the summer evenings on the porch faded away.

The creak of the wide old porch boards made JoJo crave the medicine of laughter. It'd been too long since she really, really laughed. With joy. With abandon.

Even on the summer nights with Haley and Cole, she was reserved. Still locked down.

"Hal, sorry I'm late," she called toward the grand salon as she ducked into the kitchenette, an old butler's pantry modernized while maintaining its old-world charm. She stored her handbag in the cabinet next to the wall.

"I'm upstairs." Haley's distant voice beckoned Jo past the boxes of Christmas decorations stacked by the fireplace in the grand salon toward the sprawling center staircase.

Taking the steps two at a time to the mezzanine, she found her cousin and best friend, who was pregnant with her first child, kicking a large box toward the storage room, better known as "the closet."

"Here, let me."

"It's the veils. Amber Miller's should be in this shipment. She called again to see if it had arrived." With a sigh, Haley sat in the mohair club chair in the corner under the eaves and the high portal window. "The baby is getting heavy. By the way, I've decided to just decorate the tree tonight. I'm too tired to do the whole kit and caboodle. Let's do it Saturday, after Black Friday.

I've convinced myself the brides don't care about Christmas decorations, only the dresses."

"Wise move."

"Plus, I still have the pies to bake for tomorrow. I don't suppose Aunt Lila would cotton to store bought."

JoJo shot her a wry look. "Have you met my mother?"

"Right. I didn't think so."

"If we only decorate the tree tonight, when do you want to do the rest of the shop? Saturday won't be any better than Friday."

"Hush, let me live with my fantasy."

JoJo laughed as she ran the box cutter through the packing tape. "I'll take care of the tree and staircase tonight. You go on home."

"You know I don't deserve you." Haley shifted forward, her sleek blonde hair falling over her shoulders, her hand resting on her round middle, watching JoJo sort the veils. "Nor does this town. You do so much. How did the final downtown decorating go?"

"We added twinkle lights around the lampposts this afternoon. And the park trees." JoJo sighed. "The town is so beautiful. Please, God, let it snow this Christmas."

"The predictions are for a warm Christmas."

"This weird man in purple stopped me on my way here. Said we were going to have a white Christmas but I don't think he knew what he was talking about. Anyway, I ordered a pair of beautiful white ankle boots with cloth buttons. Keep your eyes out for them. They've not arrived yet." JoJo handed the first veil to Haley. "The Bray-Lindsay is gorgeous. Almost makes *me* want to get married."

"You mean you don't? Is there something you want to tell me? Besides buying a pair of *bridal* booties you never intend to wear."

"Oh, I'm going to wear them. Just not as a bride. No one will know the difference."

"Where are you going to wear them?"

"To the Christmas Eve service. Maybe the kids' play, and under my costume for the Dickenson Carolers. Cole's company Christmas party. If I'm invited again this year. There are plenty of places to wear wedding boots besides down the aisle."

"Only you, Jo."

"I'll consider that a compliment. What do you think of the Melinda House?" JoJo raised another veil to the light falling through the portal. "The lace looks cheap."

"She's new to veils and might have cut some corners. Though she charges enough." Haley shifted in the chair, pressing on the baby. "She's sleeping on my bladder."

"Take heart. Only three months to go." JoJo unwrapped a floor-length, embroidered lace mantilla veil. "This is from Elnora. Gorgeous."

"She always has beautiful veils. Amber will be pleased. Is it cathedral length? The first one came in as a chapel."

"It's long enough."

"Try it on."

Jo glanced at her cousin then down at her slacks and sweater. "I'm not dressed for it."

"Please? I want to see the length and you're her height. It should touch the floor and trail ten feet behind you."

"I'd rather not, Haley. Trying on a veil when I'm not the bride feels..." Jo glanced in the mirror. "Feels weird. Especially when I don't intend on getting married. I don't even have a boyfriend. Besides, I'm not the bride type."

Since her first day on the job, she'd determined to never tempt her heart. Never try on a gown or veil and glance in the mirror. Why dress up for a party she'd never attend?

Black Friday would deliver the bride types. The hopeful, the curious, the wannabes. Women trying on dresses when they didn't have a ring or a promise.

JoJo didn't judge their enthusiasm, but she'd not join them.

"But you don't mind wearing bridal booties?" Haley said.

"In my mind they're just white ankle boots. And don't mess with my logic. It's precariously balanced." JoJo examined the thick tulle where the edge was trimmed with flowers in French lace. Stunning.

She'd never confessed out loud but the idea of marriage terrified her. Well, not the institution but her poor judgment in men.

"Hey." Haley reached out with her soft tone and gentle touch. "He's gone."

"Who? What are you talking about?" JoJo turned away from her cousin's knowing gaze.

"You know who I'm talking about. He's out of your life. We all make mistakes. Look at me with Dax. I had no idea he was married. After I left him, I came home to find Cole."

"I've been home five years. I'm not sure there is someone in Hearts Bend for me."

"Are you looking?"

Jo shook her head. "Were you looking?"

"Don't mess with my logic. It's precariously balanced."

"I don't trust my judgment."

"That's understandable, but you're home, with us, not alone in a big city." Haley pushed out of the chair and reached for the veil. "We'll help you."

"It takes a village to find JoJo Castle a husband?" Jo examined the veil as Haley spread it across the floor. "If Amber doesn't want it, someone will. It's beautiful."

"I agree. Hey, remember how Tammy and I used to play brides in here? You always wanted to join us."

"And you never let me."

"The difference between twelve and nine is enormous. But now look, we're the same age. And if I recall, we *did* let you play with us once. You were a bridesmaid."

"I was supposed to be a bridesmaid with a newspaper veil, but you demoted me to a guest sitting in a smelly, dusty, ripped chair."

She'd pestered Haley and her childhood best friend Tammy to let her play, following them on her bike, until they finally agreed she could sneak into the shop with them.

"Do you think of her often?" Jo said. "You were going to own this place with her."

"Not as much as I did. But when I was in the midst of the remodel or fighting to get inventory, I thought of her all the time. I'd have quit otherwise."

Tammy was supposed to be alive and working with Haley's business partner. But she lost a battle with cancer before her thirtieth birthday. Haley carried the torch of their dream into reality.

"I hope I'm a good replacement," Jo said.

"More than. And you don't have to try on the veil but I will officially promote you to a bridesmaid. You're no longer a *guest*."

Tenderness filled the pause between them.

"Oh, here, give it to me. I'll try it on. In memory of Tammy."

"Jo, no, you don't—"

"Move before I change my mind."

Before the veil made her yearn for a good man and a house with the yard and children to play in it.

Of course the world was full of good men. Daddy was a good man. So was Cole. Jo had resigned herself there just wasn't one for her.

Jo turned her back to the mirror as Haley smoothed her wild brunette wisps toward her falling ponytail and fit the headband in her hair. Then she arranged the veil around Jo's shoulders.

"Oh, Jo, I wish you'd turn around. Look in the mirror."

"No thanks. I already broke my don't-try-on rule."

"You look so lovely." Haley stepped back for a wider view, arms crossed, a smirk on her lips. "Standing there so stiff and uncomfortable."

"Remind me not to try on a veil for you in the future. Can I take it off now?"

"I'm just telling you how beautiful you are." Haley fussed and perfected the veil around Jo's shoulders. "You know, one day some *cowboy* is going to ride into town on his black steed and sweep you off your feet."

"You've been reading romance novels again."

"So what if I have? Please, one glance in the mirror."

"Nothing doing. I know your tricks. I've seen you do it on dozens of brides."

"What tricks?"

"The ones you learned from Charlotte Rose. Where you get a bride to see herself how her groom, her family, or shoot, all of heaven sees her and next thing you know, she's weeping and her mother is writing a check."

"Those are truths not tricks."

Charlotte Rose, who owned Malone & Co., a bridal shop in Birmingham, helped Haley open her shop four years ago. Even gave her some sort of magical wedding dress to wear on her own special day.

The gown came with some sort of lore. A grand tale about four brides and a dress designed in 1912 by a black seamstress for a Birmingham society girl. Ever after the gown was rumored to fit every bride who tried it on. It fit the bride no matter what her size, and looked contemporary and in-style for the decade she lived in. Even more crazy, the material, the threads, the beading and adornments never broke, faded or wore out.

Haley had recounted the dress story to JoJo as she was emerging from the dark fog of Dallas so the specifics remained vague. Only a few poetic details lingered.

She'd been at the wedding but not present. Not open to love because fear still clung every part of her.

"I'm calling Amber. I'll tell her the veil is stunning and perfect."

"Unique. Stress how this veil is one of a kind."

"Listen to you. And you called me tricky."

"One thing I learned in the PR business. Base all your exaggerations in truth. This is the only Elnora cathedral length veil with French lace in Hearts Bend, right?"

"The shop will be in good hands when I have the baby."

"Speaking of the baby. I was wondering if we could—" Jo paused when her phone jingled from her hip pocket.

The face of Uncle Ben, youngest brother to her daddy, and Haley's mama, was on the screen. He was also the wildest child of the Castle kids. Ben had lived with Daddy and Mama since he'd burned all the wax off his candle wick about ten years ago.

"Jo!" His loud voice vibrated with panicked. "Better get here. Not going to sugarcoat it, there's blood. I called 9-1-1."

"What happened?" The light faded from the closet's high portal window as a winter cloud passed over.

"Just get here."

She didn't have to be told again. JoJo bolted from the long, narrow space and sailed down the stairs. Tragedy. Right on time. At Christmas. She hated to believe in bad luck, but it seemed holiday disaster was the curse of the Reed Castle family.

"JoJo, what's wrong? Where are you going?" Haley bounced down the grand staircase behind her. "You're still wearing the veil."

But she didn't have time to answer. She grabbed her handbag from the pantry and banged out the porch door, fishing for her keys, praying the old red beater—so opposite the two-year-old Beamer she drove in Dallas—would start.

Her hands trembled as she turned the ignition. Slamming the door, she shifted into gear and shot toward First Avenue and the six-mile drive down River Road toward home.

As she turned the corner, she caught sight of Haley running from the shop's front door, her hand holding her belly. *"Jo! Veil...decorating..."*

Speeding past the town Christmas lights into the last sliver of the setting sun, Jo knew it'd been a mistake. To put on the veil. To hope. Even at Christmas, some people just couldn't find joy. And she was one.

BUCK

After ten years on the road, he was eager for a season at home. Parking under the thick, naked limbs of the oaks in Gardenia Park, Buck paused at the First Avenue light on his way to Java Jane's, Hearts Bend's favorite coffee shop.

"Buck Mathews!"

Buck waved at the disembodied voice without looking. A fan. Or maybe a friend of his parents, or an old buddy of his from high school.

He glanced at the light, waiting for his turn to cross. Hearts Bend was small and charming, hosting not one but *two* traffic lights. And First Avenue, the main drag through town, seemed busier than he ever remembered.

The walk sign gave him the go-ahead, but his step off the curb was arrested by a coughing and clattering beat-up old Datsun gunning under the red light.

The driver, without much concern for her traffic violation, wore a long, white veil. Which was caught in the door and flapping in the wind.

A runaway bride. A country song in live action. A melody spun in his head as his gazed followed the sorry-looking machine through the second light.

However, he wasn't a singer-songwriter this month. He was a son, brother, friend.

With a glance at his watch, Buck hurried across the avenue. Stokes would be waiting.

On the other side, he spotted Haley, a treasured, longtime friend who was also the wife of his good buddy Cole.

"Haley, hey."

"Buck." She drew her gaze from the street and flashed him a bright, albeit surprised smile. "Wow. You're in town." Her tone carried a thousand unspoken words.

"For the holidays, yes."

Okay, so he'd not been home much since he moved to Nashville after high school. But he had a dream to chase and sacrifices had to be made. Though lately, he wondered at the price he paid for his fame and fortune.

"One of your customers? The runaway bride?" he said.

"She wasn't a runaway bride. That was JoJo wearing an expensive veil. She told me she didn't want to try it on, but did I listen? No. Then Ben called, and she shot out of the shop like a fireball. And we have to put up the tree for Black Friday." She closed her eyes and waved off her complaints. "Never mind me. Buck Mathews, what are you doing in town?"

"Taking a break. Visiting the folks."

As it turned out, building a successful music career required every ounce of his heart, mind, body, and soul. His visits home were brief. Often full of distraction.

Yet a dozen years later with seven albums and nonstop touring he'd achieved the skyrocketing career he'd dreamed of since he was fourteen.

His effort and talent paid big dividends. Fame. Awards. Money. Lots of money.

Lately he noticed this hole, a kind of loneliness, filling the space between his heart and ribs. His personal life, with little time for his family and friends, was cold and barren. His one attempt at romance with a tech executive was short-lived and tumultuous.

But Haley? She was warm and open, kindness replacing the

surprise in her eyes. The hole in his middle drank of her presence. "I thought you'd become too famous for Hearts Bend."

"Never. You're my people."

"Then you must visit more often. Can you come into the shop?" She shivered in the cold. "I'll fix you a cup of tea. Cole's stopping by soon."

"I'd love to but I'm meeting my manager at Java Jane's."

"Then come by the house later. How long are you in town? Just for Thanksgiving?"

"Thought I'd stick around until the New Year. Eat too much turkey and too many Christmas cookies." He patted his lean belly then motioned to Haley's swelling middle. "When's he due?"

"She. Late March. We're going to call her Emily."

"Let me know where you're registered. Be sure there are big, expensive items on it."

"Don't tempt me."

"Do it." From his pocket, his phone rang, and he knew without looking it was Stokes. He answered with, "I'm on my way." Then turned to Haley. "I need to go, but I want to get with y'all for sure. I've been missing home." More than home. He'd been missing community. Love. And every nuance about Hearts Bend that had formed him.

"I'll have Cole call you." Haley glanced in the direction where the faded red car had disappeared. "By the way, did you hear me say the *runaway* was JoJo Castle?"

"I heard you." He started for Java Jane's before Stokes could call again.

"She's not engaged or anything," Haley said. "She works at the shop."

"Not really my business, Hal."

"Just thought you'd want to know."

"Get inside. It's too cold to stand here without a coat."

"You're not the boss of me."

He laughed the one block to Jane's. Did he know JoJo Castle

was in town? Last he heard she landed a big time PR job in Dallas? Worked for a swanky PR firm? No, wait, Mom did tell him she'd come home. But that was a few years ago. She stayed? As much as she loved Hearts Bend, she'd always wanted to see the world.

"Buck, where you been?" Stokes Stubbins met him with a scowl. "You make me drive all the way down here only to make me wait."

"I ran into an old friend." He made his way to the counter. "Once you taste Jane's coffee you'll be glad you came."

Stokes ordered a large Black Java from a cheery barista who was trying hard not to make a fuss over Buck. It was an unwritten Hearts Bend rule that Buck Mathews was just an ordinary dude if he was in town. When he was in town. Which was rare.

Since his career hit the tipping point he worked harder, toured more and prayed to God he'd not be a has-been before he turned forty.

On those rare occasions home at his parents' place on Ox Bottom Parkway, he slept and ate. Mom's country cooking refreshed his soul. He'd binge watched movies, played video games, and talked to Dad about the business.

When the barista handed him his herbal tea—caffeine was bad for the throat—he winked at her and pulled two tickets to his Grand Ole Opry show from his inside coat pocket.

"See you there."

"Really? No, you're joking. Really?" She muffled a squeal as she ran around to give him a hug and beg for a selfie.

Buck happily complied. His relationship with his fans was the biggest reason for his success.

He found Stokes at a secluded table in a dark corner, and after waving to his balding and retired high school math teacher, Buck joined him.

"So, what's this about?" Stokes fidgeted as if he planned to make a run for it any moment.

"My mom has cancer."

Stokes lowered his cup without taking a drink. "Since when? I never heard. Just saw your dad last week. Why didn't you tell me?"

"I'm telling you now." Because he didn't know until now. The family had kept him out of the loop.

Buck's mom wasn't just *any* mom, she was Lana Mathews, award-winning, acclaimed Nashville songwriter who'd penned ten number-one singles in the last twenty-five years. His dad, Owen, was a record label executive.

"Buck, I'm here. What do you need me to do? Move your media schedule? Most of those interviews can wait until the new year." Stokes sipped his coffee, grimaced, then took out his phone. "What's your mom's favorite store? I want to send her something."

"Stokes, it's more than interviews. I want to cancel my December shows. Mom loves flowers. Especially Christmas arrangements."

Stokes's resolute expression turned to stone. "Cancel? Your shows?"

"Yes." One nod to emphasize his point. "Turns out this is Mom's second bout. They didn't tell me the first time. But Sadie called this go-round. She thought I deserved to know."

"Well, it was the sisterly thing to do. Buck, I'm sorry about Lana, but you can't be serious about canceling. The show *must* go on. Remember when I tried to cancel the year you broke your leg skiing? You refused. Never missed one performance. Same thing when you had the flu with a 101 fever. These Christmas shows are in small, intimate venues with very rich, influential people. You can't cancel."

"I don't care. My mom has cancer, Stokes. I want to spend time with her. I don't even know the full diagnosis or what happened the first time. They didn't tell me because I was on the road. Over a decade on the road building a career and I guess I got kicked out of my own family." Buck sat back and stared at the Christmas tableau beyond the window. When had the family decided he wasn't one of them? That they could go through a crisis without him? "They thought I needed to be out there, entertaining and winning over fans. Becoming some *big* star. What does it all mean if I don't have family? If my mother is in the cold, hard ground?"

"I'm sure they would've called if—"

"She was on her deathbed? When it's too late?"

"You exaggerate. Buck, these shows are important. The label will not be happy. Don Bliss will be livid."

"Forget the label. Forget the booking agent. For the past twelve years I've done everything asked of me and more. Now it's my turn to make a request."

He had debated cancelling the shows. There were only five and he'd be gone four days tops. But the moment he crossed Hearts Bend city line, he yearned for a season of rest. To go to ground. To his roots. Be with the town and people who formed his youth.

And if JoJo was back...

Stokes tapped notes on his phone, mumbling. "I guess I could say it's a family emergency."

"No." Buck clapped his hand on Stokes's arm. "That will raise suspicion and I want to protect Mom's privacy. Tell them I need a rest. I did a hundred shows this year while recording a new album. I need a break before it starts all over again."

"You know the buzz on the album is trending. Song Tunes increased the marketing and promotion budget." Stokes smiled. He'd been in the biz for over thirty years, but Buck was his biggest and best artist. "Greg Leininger is already talking new contract."

"Then give me grace to step back this month. And maybe the next. Regroup." Too much time in the glow of the superstar limelight had dried up the core of the humble country boy who charmed the world.

Just the idea of staying close to home and lovely Hearts Bend for the holidays eased the tension in his neck. Released the knot of work-work-work from his gut.

He missed Dad, Mom, Nana and Paps, Sadie, her husband Eric, and their kids. He missed the town square and all the traditions that made this place one for the books.

Hearts Bend was the best-kept secret in the South. In fact, Buck scrubbed the name from all his bios. Never mentioned it in interviews. He was born and raised "outside of Nashville."

"Are you sure?" Stokes sighed over his coffee. "If so, I'll do my best tap dancing. It is Christmas after all. But come January, Buck, you have to start promoting the new single. It drops in March."

Buck swallowed his *We'll see* with a sip of tea. On the short walk from The Wedding Shop to Java Jane's, the desire for a break had rooted even deeper. He didn't want to hit the New Year on the run. A couple of months off sounded darn good.

Time with Mom in her music room made him exhale. He needed to be around her, her softness, her talent. Hear her words of wisdom, make memories. Ask her how to let go of all the entrapments of fame to *find a life*. Find love.

"Get Aubrey James or Tracie Blue to cover the December dates," Buck said. "They're bigger names than I am."

Aubrey had been around for almost twenty years, and Tracie charted back-to-back number ones last year.

Stokes gave him a long look. "Humble looks good on you."

"My old paps says, 'Humility is a magnet for God's affection,'" Buck said. "Don't know why I said that. Haven't thought of it in a long time."

But he needed some Divine affection on his tattered soul.

"Has a ring of truth, I suppose." Stokes made a face as he finished his coffee.

Humility had been the seed of Buck's beginning. Despite being born with Music Row's silver spoon in his mouth, he'd paid his dues like every other artist. Didn't matter he grew up with country legends at his family's dinner table. He had to wait his turn at open mike nights at the Bluebird, gigging whenever and wherever he could.

Mom taught him to write songs and Dad schooled him on the business side of music, but neither one used their influence to give him an inside track.

"So your mom," Stokes said. "Is she dying?"

"I don't think so. She has spots on her lungs. They thought they got them before. Ironic isn't it? Never smoked a day in her life."

"Lana's a fighter." Stokes leaned toward Buck. "I'll support you canceling shows but it has to stop here. Hard work and humility got you this far. It'll take you the rest of the way. But the moment you look and act like you're believing your own press, it's over."

"I know. I'm sorry about this. I like these small venues. They've been good to me. But I need to be here." For himself as much as Mom. "And I doubt I'll be missed. Private parties with very rich people who drink too much and beg me to sing 'Free Bird' in the middle of my first set is not exactly my fan base." He leaned toward Stokes and lowered his voice. "I'm thirty years old and my memories of home end when I was eighteen. The rest is a blur of tour buses, recording studios, writing sessions, and award shows."

"Some would call that living the dream."

"What happens when you wake up and find you're living it all alone?" Buck pushed back from the table. "Thanks for seeing to this."

"What about the Opry?" Stokes stood and tossed his coffee cup in the trash. "It's next week. Close to home."

"I'll play the Opry. I can drive up on next Friday, rehearse, do the show on Saturday, and be home that night."

"Home as in here? You're not even staying at your place in Nashville?"

"Home is Hearts Bend for the next month." Buck moved toward the door. "There's some people I want to get reacquainted with."

A tall brunette with vibrant green eyes to start.

Despite the cold, Buck drove to his parents' place with his window down. The chill, scented with a hint of snow and a wood fire, cleared his head. Unclogged his emotions. Unlocked memories.

Turning down his parents' trimmed and clipped driveway, his mind's eye envisioned JoJo speeding down First Avenue with her veil slapping in the wind. And he laughed. That move was *so* JoJo.

And one of the reasons he loved her.

Chapter Two

❦

JOJO

Black Friday was a madhouse. Not only was Hearts Bend bustling with tourists, but the copy Jo had written for the shop's radio promo proved effective.

She sold three dresses herself before lunch.

"Where's my veil?" Haley whispered when JoJo first arrived. She was on her way to the grand salon with the latest Elnora gown in her hands.

"Soaking."

Seems a girl couldn't drive six-plus miles with a fine tulle-and-lace veil snapping in the wind without soiling it. Plus, she *might* have stepped on it a half dozen times running into the house.

Then Saturday morning Jo arrived at the shop with gooey, iced cinnamon buns from Haven's Bakery and two steaming cups of coffee. Along with a washed-white-as-snow veil.

"Breakfast and one very clean veil." In the butler's pantry, Jo held up the Haven's box and the neatly folded veil. "Again, I'm sorry."

"Jo, you said sorry enough already." Haley inspected the lace with an expert eye. "I can't believe you got this so clean!"

"I can't believe Ben freaked out over red wrapping paper. Blood, my eye."

Haley made a face. "It's Ben, Jo. He has a knack for drama. When I told Mom he freaked out over Aunt Lila falling onto a big sheet of red wrapping paper, she said, 'That's my little brother,' and couldn't stop laughing."

"Dad said, 'Ben, do you need an eye doctor appointment?'"

The girls' laughter filled the narrow butler's pantry. "Dear Ben," Haley said.

"You can't help but love him no matter how crazy he makes you." Jo passed Haley a cinnamon roll and pointed to the decaf coffee with extra cream.

Thanksgiving Day, however, the family never said a word behind his back. Never even snickered. The Wednesday episode had come and gone. Frankly JoJo was relieved it wasn't a real Castle disaster.

But now that the holiday and Black Friday were behind them, JoJo felt Haley's unspoken query.

Why'd you run out like that?

Jo focused on filling her mouth with food and coffee, and reached for the latest bridal magazine resting on the edge of the table.

But flipping through the pages, chewing and swallowing, fidgeting and shifting, didn't do much to abate Haley's visual inquiry.

"Okay, fine. I don't know." Jo slapped the magazine closed and shoved it forward. "I just panicked. Ben made it sound like Mama was at death's door."

"This isn't the first time you've overreacted."

"I don't know what you mean." But she did, didn't she?

"You sat up all night with Uncle Reed when he had the flu."

"His fever was over a hundred."

"I asked you to go to Paris with me and you said no."

"I hear it's a dirty city these days. Not worth seeing."

"You've wanted to see Paris since we were kids."

"I thought I should stay home. Near the family."

Haley stretched her hand to Jo's. "You're scared. It's okay to admit it. It's also okay to confront it."

"I'm not scared." Only a little. Sometimes a lot. "But you know the Castle family curse."

Haley's laugh was cut short by Jo's sharp glance and stern expression. "You're serious?"

"You can't deny it. Daddy's big car accident that put him out of work for almost a year. We've never recovered from the financial loss. The trailer fire. Mama's job losses. Three in five years. Daddy's business partners stealing the company out from under him. The New Year's Eve flood of 2000."

"Bad things happen. So what? It doesn't mean the family is cursed."

"Then there was the thing. In Dallas. The week before Christmas." Speaking of it even in cloaked terms always brought her tears close.

Haley shoved out of her chair and pressed her hand on Jo's shoulder. "But you're here now. Nothing bad has happened since."

She reached for a napkin to dry her cheeks. "I wonder if I'll ever move on." How could the past so weigh a girl down?

"Try reminiscing about good times. Hey, didn't your folks get the Scott farm at Christmas?" Haley returned to her chair and breakfast Danish with a gleam in her eyes.

"Yeah, I guess so." Jo took a sip of coffee. "That *was* a lovely Christmas."

Fifteen years ago on a crisp Christmas morning the mayor and three council members came to the Castles' home on Third Street—the small cramped place they rented after the trailer fire—with the deed to the Scott farm. The bank had already approved the loan because a healthy down payment had been made by anonymous donors. All Daddy and Mama had to do was sign on the dotted line and make plans to move.

There were joyous tears all morning. Mama even started packing. After dinner they all drove out to the Scott farm where Daddy's elderly aunt Cora lived in the '30s. (Daddy and Aunt Joanne didn't even know about her until they were much older.) The three of them stood on the bank of the river and praised God.

And it seemed circumstances *did* turn around for Daddy and Mama. Then five years later Daddy's business partners betrayed him, and he'd walked with a limp ever since.

"Don't tell my mother," Haley said, "but I wish we celebrated all family holidays at your house. Uncle Reed has fixed it up so lovely. And the sound of the river at night is so peaceful. We have such good times on the back porch or picnicking under the trees. It's like my second home."

"We finished decorating last night. The place is magical."

"That's it, I'm telling Mom we're going to Aunt Lila's for Christmas dinner. I don't care if it's her turn to host. I'll invite my brothers. And Cole's mom and brothers too."

Jo squeezed Haley's hand. "Thank you. For making me remember the good."

Haley bent to kiss her forehead. "Come on, we have a shop to decorate." She took a bite of her Danish, then moved to the sound system tucked under the cabinets. "I'll put on some Bing and we can believe for a marvelous, miraculous, glorious Christmas season."

"I'm sorry I bugged out on you Wednesday. I should've come back when I knew Mama was okay." A shallow tear crested the corner of Jo's eye. But the ordeal had jump-started her nerves and the memory of Dallas. So she'd stayed tucked inside the womb of her parents' home.

"Forget it. Cole helped me with the tree. We got it done in no time. He stacked all the decoration boxes along the far mezzanine wall. Let me put this veil away and we can get going."

Jo finished her last bite of breakfast and followed Haley through the grand salon to the stairs. Haley was right. She should think of positive things. How blessed she was to have Daddy and Mama, Hearts Bend, working with her cousin and friend, and a safe place to hide when the world became terrifying.

"I'll call Amber about the veil." Haley unlocked the closet. "Then we'll finish decorating the small salon and staircase. Then set out the caroler statues."

"Sounds good. Haley, I've been thinking about the shop, developing a brand and—"

"Interesting. So have I." Haley glanced back at her. "Let's sit down in January and talk. I've been doing well on my own the last four years, but it's time to think about the future. Since I have a public relations genius in the house..."

"Don't know about genius, but I have some ideas." Lots of ideas. She was relieved Haley had been thinking about things too.

"You're a genius. You handled the reputation of that arrogant NFL player. What's his name?"

"Calvin Blue. And he's not so arrogant. Just got swept into wrong company. He was too naïve and too rich for his own good." Jo's attention landed on a glowing, almost glistening wedding gown draped over a dress form in the front left corner. Light from the windows flowed toward the silk folds and lingered in the threads. "He's actually turned around his reputation. Texted me last week with an update on his inner-city program. Haley, when did you get this gown? It's stunning."

"What gown?" Haley turned from the veil wardrobe. "Oh mercy, that's my wedding dress. How did it get here? I stored it in the trunk four years ago."

"Not me. So, this is *the* dress?"

"You don't remember?"

"Not really. I was still in a fog from Dallas at your wedding."

Jo touched an angled, bell sleeve. The material was beautiful with a silky sheen and sweetheart neckline. The dress seemed to breathe with a life of its own. "So *this* is the ancient wedding gown from 1912." She knelt to inspect the seams, the material, and to look for any blemish. How could a dress so old be so fresh and beautiful?

How did it seem to *speak* to her? Turning over the V-cut hem, she found a neatly stitched TH.

"Taffy Hayes," Haley whispered over her shoulder. "She was the black seamstress who sewed the gown for a very *nouveau riche* Birmingham society family. Emily Canton married Daniel Ludlow and became Charlotte's great-grandmother. But she never knew anything about Emily or her family until she found the dress in an old trunk. It sent her on quite the journey."

"And the journey ended with you." Jo gazed up at Haley.

"I guess so. I felt unworthy, yet honored, to be invited into the unique sisterhood of the dress. Like, why me?" Haley began to remove the dress from the form. "But the moment I put it on, all my guilt and shame, especially over Dax, melted away. I could barely remember how I felt when I found out he was married. I could look at myself square in the eye for the first time in years. I knew this dress was special. If Charlotte was offering it to me, I was going to take it. I don't know how it got out, but I'm putting it away. I don't want it damaged. I feel responsible, you know, to protect it for the next hundred-plus years. To guard the stories of the other brides. Help me, Jo. Open the trunk under the window. See the linen bag? The dress goes inside."

Jo pulled the drawstrings on the cream-colored sack. "If you didn't get it out, who did?"

"I have no idea. Marla?" The part-time college student worked a few hours a week. "But she shouldn't be up here. Yesterday was a zoo, though. I estimated we had three hundred walk through the door."

"But it was worth it at the end of the day. We had, what, ten sales?"

As quaint and remote as Hearts Bend remained over the years, digging deep roots in the shade of Nashville, it had become something of a holiday tourist destination.

The picturesque town with its brick streets and Victorian streetlamps and live carolers in the park was a page out of Dickens.

"What's the significance of the bag and the trunk?" Jo knelt next to Haley as she snapped the lock. The shining, relatively new brass hasp with lock and key seemed out of place on the otherwise battered and worn steamer.

"Charlotte discovered the dress in the trunk when she bought it at an auction on Red Mountain. You should hear her tell the story. 'Here I am, bidding on a trunk I do not want. But dollar amounts kept flying out of my mouth.'" Haley's laugh was sweet. "Anyway, according to legend—"

Jo leaned back against the wall, arms folded on top of her raised knees, and listened.

"—the bride before Charlotte, Hillary, also found the dress in the trunk, hidden away in her family's basement. The bride before her was the daughter of a mine worker who worked in a Birmingham department store. She inherited the dress firsthand from Emily." Haley stored the trunk key in the middle drawer of the old secretary tucked against the western wall.

"I don't get it. Why the mystery? Why the trunk? Just put the dress out to be selected by the bride who wants it."

"I'm not sure I can." Haley rested one hand on the baby. For a split second Jo ached to know what her cousin knew. The feeling of life growing inside. A little person with fingers and toes, a nose, a soul, a spirit. "There seems to be a charge to the last bride to find the next."

"And how are you handling that charge?"

"I'm not." Haley made a face as she glanced at the trunk. "Charlotte promised that when I decided who the next bride was to be, the dress would fit."

"Then we know it's not me."

"Really? We know no such thing."

"Sure, I can tell by looking it wouldn't fit me. I'm too tall. Too wide. That dress is for a 1912 woman in a corset."

Jo shoved off the floor with her eye on Haley's desk where a row of photos in engraved antique frames told the story of each bride and groom. She'd seen these images dozens of times but never really paused to look.

The first was Emily and Daniel leaving the church on the back of a horse. Now there was an untold story. A society bride on the back of a horse? But the love in their expressions? Enviable. She was beautiful, and he was handsome.

Jo had never known a love like the one she saw on their faces. Not a two-sided one anyway. She'd loved someone. Once. Up close but yet so far. He'd never noticed her. Not in *that* way. But that was years ago. She'd not seen him since she moved to Dallas.

The next frame was of Mary Grace and Thomas walking down the aisle of a church. He was rugged looking with Appalachian features and wearing a plain suit. She, in the wedding dress, walked out of the picture and into Jo's heart.

"Mary Grace died last year at a hundred and two."

JoJo glanced back at Haley. "What life she must have seen."

The next frame bore the names Hillary and Joel. A gorgeous, sexy, 1960s couple. She with her long blonde hair and flower wreath. He so regal and grand in his Marine uniform, chiseled chin, and piercing gaze. Jo suddenly ached to know them.

"These two had quite a passion," she said, more to herself than Haley.

"He was killed in Nam. I met Hillary right after my wedding when I went down to see Charlotte. The three of us went to see Mary Grace. It was quite a special day. I cried so much Cole thought I was dehydrated."

The next picture was of Charlotte and Tim. Another stunning couple. Last but not least, Haley and Cole. Also beautiful and handsome. Happy. In love. Perfectly matched.

"I'm guessing to wear this dress the bride has to be drop-dead gorgeous and engaged to a stunningly handsome groom."

"Hardly." Haley swatted at her shoulder. "But if the dress thinks you're beautiful, then I suppose you are."

Jo examined each picture up close. "No two are alike. The brides, I mean. Different sizes and shapes. It even looks different on each of you. Like a bespoke design."

"It's part of the mystery. It has fit every woman who's tried it on."

"I guess we should get to decorating," Jo said, the images, the conversation pricking at her in a way she couldn't describe. "The shop opens in an hour."

"Right. Let's get as much done as we can. If we don't do it up like years past, I'm okay with it. Marla's coming in at twelve since we'll be busy today and I've ordered pizza for lunch." Haley started for the door then paused. "Jo, do you seriously not have any romantic dreams?"

Jo crossed the mezzanine without answering. "I'll grab this big box if you want to get the smaller one."

"What if I fix you up with a really great guy? Cole's friend—"

"Stop. No."

"But, Jo, you can't—"

"Can't what? Be afraid? Yes, I can. Now let's go."

Jo descended the stairs to the soothing voice of Bing singing of a silent night. She commanded the smart device to turn on the Christmas lights, then opened the box full of garland.

The cousins worked diligently until Haley opened the shop. Customers were already waiting on the sidewalk.

At noon, Marla and the pizza arrived. JoJo followed Haley and the glorious aroma of cheese and warm dough to the butler's pantry. Cole entered the back door just as they set the large box on the table.

"Look who I found wandering the streets."

JoJo sank into the nearest chair as Buck Mathews stepped around her cousin-in-law.

"Buck, just in time for pizza." Haley passed him, and Cole, a paper plate and napkin. "Drinks are in the fridge."

"Buck, what's you're pleasure?" Cole stepped with his wife toward the fridge leaving JoJo to face *him* alone. The one she'd loved who never knew she existed. Not in that way.

"Sweet tea, if you have it. Hello, Jo."

"Buck. It's been a long time." She sounded cold. But she didn't mean to sound cold. She was just... Cold. Shivering from the inside out.

Since returning to Hearts Bend five years ago, she'd not seen him in town at all. Though she heard he'd visited.

"It has. Too long."

He was as handsome as ever, though more like a man than the boy she remembered, his face and body filled out. He moved with the confidence and swagger that came from achieving all his dreams before turning thirty. Yet in the midst of his success, he emanated a hometown, boy-next-door charm.

It was why *People* magazine called him America's Sexiest Sweetheart.

"You look good," he said, low, his gaze fixed on her.

"Y-you too." She ran her hand over her hair, smoothing down the frays loose from her ponytail.

"Buck." Cole slapped a cold bottle of golden tea against his chest. "I brought one for you too, Jo."

"Th-thank you."

"I never remember to take selfies, but I'm taking one today," Haley said, setting down a bottle of water. "All my besties right here. Jo, can we post this on our social media sites? Sorry, Buck, I'm shamelessly exploiting our friendship."

"My publicist will be swamped with questions about my upcoming wedding." Even his laugh sounded like a song.

It was well known that Buck Mathews limited social media to his career, keeping his private life quiet.

"You know what they say." Cole set one arm on Buck's shoulder and another around his wife's waist. "No such thing as bad press."

"*They* don't know what they're talking about." Buck glanced toward Jo. "What are you doing over there? Get in here."

She'd been clinging to the wall, heart swirling, resenting the way *he* made her feel. Weak and wobbly. Girly and giddy. How did he have *any* power over her after all these years? They weren't teens sitting on the rooftop outside her bedroom window talking until dawn.

"Hurry up, Jo." Haley handed her phone to Cole when he insisted her arms were too short. "I'm starved and the pizza is getting cold."

"Jo?" Buck beckoned her. She hesitated, then moved in under his arm, trembling when he clapped his hand around her waist.

"Say 'weddings.'" Cole snapped the picture.

Buck suggested a goofy one, so they all posed like an outlaw gang, and the fun eased JoJo's jitters.

"Send me copies," he said. "I'll have my team post on my sites, give the shop a plug." Buck's hand remained around Jo as the four of them huddled to see the image. And her shivers warmed to a small inferno.

When Haley handed her phone to Jo to post the images on the shop's accounts, the huddle broke and moved toward lunch.

"Buck, want to help decorate?" Haley said. "Cole's going to Nashville for supplies. We could use a bit of muscle around here."

"I'm your guy." He Popeyed his arm, revealing a toned, well-formed bicep.

Meanwhile Jo posted the images and munched on her pizza, resenting her quick glance at Buck's arm. A single muscle couldn't woo her, but one muscle attached to Buck Mathews made her want things she couldn't have. Like touching him. Kissing him. Pillowing her head on his chest.

Had nothing changed in fifteen years? From the moment she clapped eyes on him in ninth grade until now, she'd loved

Buck Mathews. Loved? No, liked. Just liked. As a friend. She should be over him. Given over to adult, grown-up emotions. This teenybopper moment was just a lapse in judgment.

She was quiet most of lunch yet managed to laugh and comment at all the right moments. Then Cole kissed Haley and headed out while Buck bundled up the trash and hauled it outside.

"Oh my gosh." Haley pounced on Jo. "You're still in love with him."

"Still? I never—"

"You've *always* loved him. I never realized how much until this moment, but your expression... Jo, tell him."

"Tell him? You *are* outside your mind." She turned for the grand salon. "I'm off to decorate, you crazy, kooky cousin."

"Then I'll tell him. You two would be great together."

Jo whirled around. "If you say *anything* I'll never speak to you again. For real."

"Jo and Buck, sitting in a tree—"

JoJo clapped her hand over Haley's mouth, but her laughter and song leaked through.

"Be quiet, he's coming." She released Haley and fixed a smile for Buck.

"What can I do to help?" he said, hands on his lean waist, glancing between the cousins.

"Bring down the caroling statues and set them up outside. Jo can help. I'll relieve Marla so she can have some pizza."

"I'll show you where they are, Buck." Jo started for the stairs with a warning glance at Haley. *I mean it.*

Nevertheless, her cousin walked on sacred, secret truths. Buck was indeed the man JoJo had loved since ninth grade. But how could she still? No, it was just too crazy to consider.

She'd watched the career he'd dreamed about skyrocket and break records while she trudged to journalism, marketing, and public relations classes at Vanderbilt.

When the job offer came from a large Dallas firm, she was excited. Finally, her turn to accomplish goals and live her dream. There she'd met someone else, a dynamic, charismatic man, and move on from a silly high school crush.

But now that he stood two feet from her, nothing had changed. The man who'd set the world on fire with his velvet voice and rocking guitar was the same boy who'd set her heart ablaze all those years ago.

BUCK

Ever since he'd known her, JoJo Castle carried a bit of sadness in her green eyes. At first he thought she was just a snob. Like the other pretty girls.

Then he was paired with her for a science project in high school. She was a sophomore and he a wise junior.

They were discussing rock sediment when he saw the spark of brilliant moonlight in her otherwise shadowed eyes. He wanted to be her friend then and he wanted to be her friend now.

But based on her earlier greeting, she wasn't much interested in him.

"Do they really sing?" he said, carrying one of the male statues out the front door into the cold and setting it on a small patch of yard. Jo placed the howling dog at his feet.

"No, but Haley pipes Christmas music through those speakers." Jo pointed to small white boxes under the eaves.

"How long have you worked here?"

"Four years."

"What happened to Dallas?"

She raised her head from where she situated a singing girl. "How did you know I was in Dallas?"

He made a face. "Small town, Jo. Mom keeps me informed."

"I missed home."

"Didn't you have a dream job with a large public relations firm?"

"Wow, she really keeps you informed."

"Did you discover wedding dresses were your true calling?"

She laughed and he loved the sound. "Not really. I just wanted to come home. Then I started working for Haley and fell in love with the business."

"The girl who wanted to see the world is happy staying home?"

"Yes." She started for the door. "I'll bring down the last two carolers."

"I'll get them." Buck dashed inside ahead of her. "I'll be right back."

It'd been a long time since he'd seen her. Since his second album and her senior year at Vanderbilt. Yet he felt as if he'd spoken to her last week. Like he could bear his heart if she wanted to hear.

"Here we go." He set up the man with the conductor's wand and the second woman, who seemed to be singing with all her might.

Jo adjusted the ensemble, then called Haley out for inspection. Arms crossed against the cold, she made a quick inspection.

"Perfect. I declare the outside Christmas decorating done. Well, after Cole puts up the lights. Thank you." Haley's gaze lingered on Buck a little longer than necessary. When their eyes met she tipped her head toward Jo. He shook his head.

Don't think she's interested.

"Why don't you two go for hot chocolate at Ella's?" Haley said. "Bring back one for Marla and one for me. But take your time. No rush."

"What? We're busy today," Jo said. "I can't leave."

"Marla and I can handle it. Jo, you've worked so hard. Take a break. I like my cocoa with lots of whipped cream." Haley jogged up the steps and into the shop. "Go. I mean it."

"Buck, sorry, she's a bit crazy. She seems to think there's a spark between us." Jo made a face and rolled her eyes. "Pregnancy hormones."

"But there's not."

"I don't think so, do you? I mean, I've not seen you in, what, seven years?"

"Something like that, yeah. But, um, I'm open for hot chocolate. Haven't had a cup of Ella's in a long time."

He'd grown up sitting on one of the counter stools with his best friend, Cole, whose mother, Tina, owned the place. She'd kept them fed with hamburgers and fries all through high school.

"Really, Buck, you don't have to go. I'm sure you've got better things to do."

"Not really, but don't feel obligated."

Buck had learned to hold things loosely while on the road to fame. He'd love to talk with Jo over hot chocolate, but if she wasn't into it, then he'd move on.

A group of women passed on the sidewalk. One glanced back at him and slowed her steps.

"Hey," she whispered. "Isn't that—"

Caught. Recognized. "Come on, darling." He hooked his arm through Jo's and escorted her across the street toward Ella's Diner. "Play along. Call me Steve or something."

She laughed, skipping along beside him under the gray sky.

"What are you doing, *Steve?*"

"Those women recognized me."

"You should worry if they didn't." She glanced back. "They're still staring."

"Walk faster." Buck lengthened his stride.

"I feel like I'm running from the bad guys."

"I don't want my time home to be about me and fame. Or to steal attention from anyone. Especially Haley and the shop. She's worked hard."

"Um, dude, you bring good attention to the shop. To the

whole town. Wait until the post on Instagram goes viral. By the way, that was nice of you."

"Every once in a while I like a good selfie with friends."

At Ella's he held the door for her, feeling a bit of, well, pride to walk into one of his hometown's most treasured establishments with one of Hearts Bend's most beloved daughters.

Since he'd been home, he'd heard her name whispered at the café. At the market when he ran an errand for Mom. Walking past the Kids Theater when two city workers were hanging the sign for the Christmas play.

"Buck!" A chorus of voices greeted them. A guitar player in the corner started playing Buck's latest hit, *"Don't You Know?"*

Tina Danner scampered toward them, pointing to an open booth. "Aren't we honored? Our hometown hero is home."

"I'm not a hero." He'd played for the real heroes on four USO tours. "But it is good to be back."

"Jo, good to see you. Cole said y'all were decorating the shop. Two hot chocolates? It's getting cold out. Weatherman says we could hit freezing tonight."

"Sounds good on all accounts. And two more to go when the time comes," Buck said. "How about a plate of your hottest, most delicious fries?"

"Chocolate and fries coming up." Tina sashayed away, calling to the kitchen. "We've got country royalty in the house."

Jo made a face. "Pizza, hot chocolate, and fries on the same day? Do you want me to fit in my jeans tomorrow?"

Buck winked at her. "I think you'll fit just fine. But I hear you. Tomorrow, salads only."

She curled her lip, and he laughed. "I was just thinking I'd have one less Christmas cookie. Mama is baking today."

Despite Tina's bodacious announcement, the diner customers left him alone. A few gawked. But most of the table dwellers were old-timers who'd known Buck since he was knee-high to a grasshopper.

He waved at Bill Summers, who faced him two booths away. Bill was his first guitar teacher.

"Thanks for your help this afternoon," Jo said. "I know it meant a lot to Haley."

"I had fun." A subtle peace settled over him. Like it used to when he was in her company. "Felt good to do something for someone else."

"Did you know Tina was on the *Food Channel's Dining with Joy?*"

"I did. My girlfriend—" He paused, flipping his gaze up to JoJo. "*Ex*-girlfriend was watching the show and heard her name. She met Tina when we came to see Mom and Dad last year."

"You were in town?"

"Briefly." To introduce his future wife to his parents. "I didn't call because—"

"You don't have to explain to me."

"I thought I was going to marry her."

"I see."

"But she wasn't the one." Buck turned the napkin-wrapped flatware in his hand. "Just seemed like the next thing to do. Career success achieved. On to wife and kids."

See how easy it was to talk to Jo? As if they'd never been apart. Lived different lives.

"What happened?"

"You mean you didn't hear on the news?"

"Believe it or not, my sun doesn't rise and set on the life of Buck Mathews."

He laughed. "Good to know. Another man happened."

"She cheated on *you?*"

He loved her emphasis on *you*. "I'm better off. We eventually parted on good terms. Looking back, I can't believe I ever thought she was for me. I should've realized when she mocked Hearts Bend after our visit."

"Absolutely she wasn't the woman for you." Jo sat back as Tina delivered two giant mugs of hot chocolate, each topped with a mountain of whipped cream.

"Fries coming up."

Buck exchanged a glance and a grin with Jo. "Where do we begin?"

"I just stir the whipped cream in." She extracted a spoon from her napkin roll and stirred. "Why'd you think she was the one?"

"Good question." Buck mimicked her spoon move, then nodded at a couple of gawking tourists who paused to stare on their way to the counter. In the far corner, the guitar player started another one of his songs. "She was gorgeous and sweet. We had a lot of the same friends. I was ready for a relationship. Feeling the loneliness of the road."

The honest confession didn't sound so pitiful when he shared it with JoJo.

"You'll find the right girl. Hang in there." The platitude irritated him. In high school Jo had been the friend who gave him solid, honest wisdom.

Reading him was her superpower back in the day. When he climbed the maple tree outside her bedroom and tapped on the glass, she knew what was bugging him before his first word. If she didn't, she listened until he'd exhausted himself. Then in a simple sentence, she quelled his fear or envy, anger or hurt. Sometimes they just pondered the big questions of life together.

Man, he missed her.

"What about you? Why the escape from The Wedding Shop with your wedding veil flapping in the breeze?"

She set her mug on the table and wiped cream from her lips. "You saw that?"

"I was meeting my manager at Java Jane's."

"It wasn't my veil. I was trying it on for Haley. One of our picky customers ordered it and she wanted to see what it looked like. Then Ben called with this panicked message about Mama falling. 'There's blood.' So I ran out."

"What happened? Is she all right?"

"She's fine. Mama stumbled backward off a ladder and smacked her hand on the wall, then tripped and landed on shining red wrapping paper. Ben heard the thump, came running in to see Mama in a pool of *red*."

"Good ol' Ben."

"Scared me half to death. Mama and I gave Ben the business afterward. His weak justification was a comedy show."

He loved the lightness of her laugh.

"So everyone at the Castle house is good?"

"We are. Daddy works with Cole, which he loves."

"He's a skilled carpenter. Cole's lucky to have him."

"Mama's finally in a good position, with the school board." Jo cupped her hands around her mug. "We all love living in the ole Scott house. Did you know Mama used to ride her bike past the place as a kid and dream of living there? Though with the Castle family luck, never imagined she'd have a snowball's chance of owning it."

"Come on, you still don't believe in the Castle family curse?"

They'd fallen into their routine. Buck telling her his problems, then being a steadying force for hers.

In Buck's mind, the Castles were one of the happiest families he'd ever known. Wasn't anything for Reed Castle to have a carport full of guitar players on a Friday or Saturday night picking and grinning.

"Yes. No. I don't know. Ever since Ben called, I have a knot in my middle, waiting for something to really go wrong. Things have been good for too long. At least for Mama and Daddy."

"Just your folks? Not you?"

She took a long sip from her mug. "Enough about me. How are you, Mr. Big Time Country Superstar?"

"Good. Really good." His pat answer sounded hollow and flat in his ears.

"Hot plate of fries for my favorite country singer. Sorry it took so long. They weren't cooked to my satisfaction."

Buck sat back as Tina lowered a platter of steaming, golden potatoes. He thanked her then shoved the ketchup toward Jo.

For a few minutes, they ate in silence, dipping fried potatoes in a pile of ketchup and attempting to wash it all down with warm cocoa.

When Jo's latest sip left her with another small white mustache, Buck reached across with his napkin. "You could pull off a 'stache if you wanted."

"Heaven help me. Though Granny sported a good one in her eighties. Behold my future."

"My granddad had a beard coming out of his ears. Behold *my* future. We'd make a good pair, no?"

"A regular circus act." But when he looked at her, she was sober, despite the soft pink hue covering her cheeks. "So, tell me, why are you in town?"

"Mom. Seems the family didn't want me to know she was dealing with tumors in her lungs. But Sadie called me this time."

"They didn't tell you? Doesn't sound like your parents." Jo started to reach for his hand but pulled back. "Don't worry, your mom is strong. A fighter."

"She is, but leaving me out was like being kicked out of the family. Sadie actually said they didn't want to interrupt my tour. Forget the tour. I'd rather be with Mom, know she's okay. What if something happened to her, and I didn't get home in time?"

Just recalling his conversation made him mad all over again. This time, however, he informed the entire Mathews clan he'd not be kept in the dark again about any family news.

"She made it through the first time and she will again. Though I'm sorry they didn't tell you. No wonder you didn't come home."

"People were wondering?"

"Maybe a few gossiping ninnies. Mama mentioned it. I was still in Dallas." She seemed to regret her last confession.

"Now we're back to you, Jo. Why'd you leave Dallas?" He felt her silence. The rhythm of her untold story.

"I told you, it was time. I missed home." The familiar sadness bloomed in her eyes and smothered the spark of moon glow.

"No boyfriend? Husband prospect?"

"Nope." She shook her head and munched on a fry.

"Why do I get the feeling there's more to the story?" There, he said it.

"How long are you staying this time?" Jo smiled up at Tina as she refilled their water glasses.

"For the holidays. Taking a break," he said.

"Do you like it, Buck? Being out there, singing in front of stadiums? Touring? Is it what you thought?"

"Performing live is amazing." He sat back as the pleasure of his confession rose in his chest "It's my favorite part about the job. It's everything I thought and more. Though in some ways, it's less. Of course, I knew a lot of the pitfalls from my parents. Dad made sure I had a good team around me. What about you? Is life turning out like you dreamed? Let's see, you wanted to backpack through Europe. See Paris, London, and Vienna."

She waved him off. "Just a bunch of silly talk." She glanced at her watch. "I really should get back. Haley likes to get off her feet for an hour in the afternoon. Tina, can we have those to-go hot chocolates?"

Buck cupped his hand over hers. "Jo, is everything all right?"

"Of course." She withdrew her hand and peered out the window, toward the park. "And since you asked, I love the wedding business. I'm going to ask Haley if I can buy into The Wedding Shop. I haven't brought it up yet, so don't say anything to her or Cole."

"From what I hear you're Miss About Town."

"I do what I can. Give back, serve on some committees, offer my PR experience."

"But no Paris, no London?"

"I have Hearts Bend. What more do I need? There's no place like home."

Tina brought the to-go hot chocolates, and Buck insisted on paying. He dropped a fifty on the table, then asked Jo to wait while he visited with the guitarist. He deposited a folded green bill in the tip jar, spoke to the man who beamed, then met her at the door.

"What are you doing tonight? Can I buy you a proper dinner?"

"Sorry, I'm back at the shop then off to the Kids Theater for the Christmas play."

"Don't tell me you're directing."

"No, not this year. But I want to make sure everything goes well for the first practice. We need to sort out the sets and costumes. Well, you know, you were in the play a couple of times."

"A couple? My granny volunteered me for every role from Baby Jesus to a wise man. When I was thirteen I rebelled. No more." He shrugged against the cold as he zipped his jacket. "It's going to snow."

"I hope so." Jo balanced the cup caddy in one hand and stuck out the other. "Thanks for the chocolate and fries. It was good to see you."

"You too." So, they were reduced to chitchat and a handshake.

She took a couple of steps backward toward First Avenue. "See you around, singing cowboy."

"See you around, girl on the rooftop."

Buck waited until she'd crossed the street before heading to his black Range Rover parked along the square. Coming home was the right decision. He needed his hometown's embrace, the joy and excitement of Christmas, and the voice of JoJo Castle resonating in his heart.

Chapter Three

◈

JOJO

Buck was on her mind as she closed the shop, as she faced the cold trek across town to the Kids Theater when her car refused to start.

He was so kind and sweet, generous, masculine, and sexy. Yes. Sexy. And it bothered her how much she liked him, let alone the heart palpitations whenever she thought of him. It was going to be a long December.

"Jo, good, you're here." A flustered and red-faced Brandi Walsh met her in the middle of the refurbished warehouse, clipboard in hand. "Ami-Jean resigned. I knew she was all wrong for the job, but no, the committee said give her a chance. Now what? She promised she could handle it. But nooooo. Who's going to step up this late? Arrange for someone to write the original song? We always have an original song. It's tradition." Brandi clucked and fussed, elbows out, bouncing up and down, her round cheeks flushed. "My blood pressure is through the roof."

"What happened?" Jo glanced at her phone. She'd texted Daddy to see if he could pick her up at the theater but so far, no response.

"Your guess is as good as mine. She probably stubbed her toe or something. Broke a nail," Brandi continued in her flustered state. "Or she may have, I think, perhaps, thought I was overbearing."

You don't say. "Then why don't you direct?" JoJo walked toward the stage, where the volunteer crew had pulled out the set and costumes.

The manger looked beat-up and in need of a refresh. The stuffed lambs were losing their insides. That would never do. But the costumes had been refurbished last year by Mrs. Manwaring and her Sewing Hens.

"I couldn't possibly. I'm directing the high school play and the community choir." She slapped her hand to her forehead and swooned onto the nearest chair. "I guess we have to cancel. I can't get anyone experienced at this late date."

"Cancel the kids' Christmas? Do you want to be run out of town? The parents count on play practice to do their Christmas shopping."

"Well this year they'll have to trust in Santa Claus to bring their little tykes presents, because I cannot handle one more thing. Rex said he'd divorce me if I volunteered for anything else." With a heaving sigh and much drama, Brandi dropped her head and ever so slowly raised the clipboard toward Jo. "Unless *you* want to direct the play."

"Me? I did my bit the last two years."

"And *what* a good bit it was, Jo."

"I'm as busy as you." And Buck was in town. There, she admitted it to herself. Seeing him for the first time in eons was like a cup of Tina's hot chocolate. Warm and satisfying. Comforting. Delicious.

On the off chance she ran into him again and he asked her to hang out, she wanted to say yes.

When she'd returned to the shop this afternoon, Haley grilled her about his offer of dinner. Jo downplayed it all, but in secret, she wished she'd said yes.

After all, he was leaving after Christmas. And she was staying. What harm could come from one dinner? It wasn't like she'd really crush on him all over again. Or that he had any intention toward her other than friendship.

Buck was the guy who never happened for her. They were not a match made in heaven.

"Jo, please. If they run me out of town, I'm taking you with me." Brandi raised the clipboard a bit higher. "Besides, you can't be as busy as me."

"I'm in the choir, a member of the carolers, on the town decorating committee, the Christmas Eve Walk coordinator, and—"

"I'll let you off choir practice, and the carolers never practice, though I told Emily Sue to rehearse at least once. The town decorating is done, and the Christmas Eve Walk takes care of itself."

"I also have a job."

"There are only four play practices. The whole thing will be over before you can sing 'Jingle Bells.'"

"Mama fell and hit her head." Well, it was something.

"I saw her at the market. She said Ben freaked out over dark red wrapping paper or something." Brandi shoved the clipboard with the schedule and script into Jo's arms. "She bragged how she hosted thirty-two at the house for Thanksgiving and ended the night with line dancing. Everything's there. You know the routine. You'll do great."

"Brandi, I can't. I don't want to do this."

"You'll have a dickens of a time with Jordan Walburg as Joseph. This is your first year with him. He played Baby Jesus eight years ago and somehow thinks he really is God Almighty. Playing Jesus's dad is like a demotion. But his mother made him try out. Anyway, if he figures out Jesus's real dad is *the* actual Lord God, you'll have chaos."

"Then why'd you choose him?"

Brandi dug in her purse. "He fit the costume. Little Paylor Perkins is Mary. What a doll. Now, she *could* be the mother of our Lord. Here's the keys to the front door and the prop room. We're a bit behind since Thanksgiving was so late. But first practice is Tuesday at four."

"Brandi—"

"And remember to have those snacks. They'll be hungry after school."

"I can see why Ami-Jean felt a little run over." A few pages of the old script escaped and fluttered to the floor.

"Righty-o. I'm out. Rex will be wanting his supper, though I don't know who broke his arm. He can open a can of soup as good as me. Don't forget the *original* song. Ta-ta."

The side door opened and closed with a *clack*, and Jo was alone. Taking a moment to collect herself, she spread the contents in her arms across the front of the stage.

Pulse pounding a bit, she skimmed the schedule and the cast. Sixteen in the cast and seven on the crew. All volunteers.

But what to do about the song? Tradition demanded a new and *original* song. With so many songwriters and musicians in town, often casualties of Music Row, the play started with a unique piece. Granny June, a gospel music old-timer and a Hearts Bend treasure, wrote most of the songs. Everyone called her Granny June even though she'd had no children of her own.

In the nineties, a former Music Row producer made a compilation album of her best songs.

Then Granny June passed on the year before JoJo's directorial debut. She never had time to hunt down someone to write a new song, so she dug out two from the eighties. So far, no one called her on it.

The side door of the theater opened. Brandi had returned. "By the way, don't think you got away with using two songs from the eighties." She pointed to her eyes then swung two fingers toward Jo. "I'm onto you. Original, Jo, original."

"Not if I don't have time."

"Find time. Hire someone. Land a'mighty, Lana Mathews lives here. Ask her." The door clattered shut.

Ask Buck's mom? She couldn't. An award-winning songwriter didn't lend her talents for free. Nor should she. Daddy always preached a laborer was worthy of his hire. Mrs. Mathews was most definitely worthy of hire. And Hearts Bend couldn't afford her. Besides, she was dealing with more serious matters!

The sliding doors on the back of the stage rattled open, and an oversized Ram truck backed in, the bed loaded with hay bales.

Sam Morris jumped from behind the wheel. "You in charge, Jo? Where do you want the hay?"

"Where it always goes. In the manger." JoJo joined Sam by his truck as he tossed the first bale to the floor.

"I thought you did your bit with the play the last two years."

"Ami-Jean quit."

"I saw that coming."

"And you didn't warn me?"

Sam grinned as he kicked off another hay bale. "I heard you had coffee with Buck Mathews at Ella's."

"Word travels fast. And it was hot chocolate."

"How long is he in town?"

"For the season, I guess."

"You two an item?"

Jo recoiled, affixing her most dubious expression. "Why would we be? We're friends."

"I thought you two liked each other."

"What? No. Never."

Sam had been a classmate of hers. A year behind Buck. Someone she'd barely talked to in the school halls, let alone told the deepest secrets of her heart.

As he dumped the last hay bale onto the stage and broke off the twine, Jo made up her mind. To move on in life, she had to leave Buck firmly in her past.

He belonged to the world. She belonged to Hearts Bend. They were on completely different journeys with no intersections.

And one day, if she were so blessed, and if she learned to trust again, she'd find a good man who belonged to Hearts Bend as much as she. They'd buy a fixer-upper and raise a couple of kids far away from any terrors that might await her in cold, black shadows.

BUCK

He had to be honest. It seemed a bit creepy to sit parked outside the Kids Theater in a dark Range Rover with tinted windows, waiting.

But he'd run into Reed Castle when he arrived at his folks. He'd been fixing some rotted deck board out back by the pool.

"Seems Jo's car won't start. Can you fetch her from the Kids Theater? I'll get that rusty bucket towed to Al's."

He said yes before Reed finished his question. Then felt the heat of being too eager with a father about his daughter.

Watching the theater door, he hoped he hadn't missed her. Hoped she'd not gone out another door. Found a ride home.

After their cocoa at Ella's, he felt a peace he'd not experienced in a long time. A rest. Like before the craziness of his career took over.

When a cut of yellow light cracked the darkness, Buck hopped out of his car. "Jo?"

She turned toward him. "Buck? What are you doing here? Thanks, Sam. See you later."

"Your dad was at the house when I got home. He said you needed a ride."

"What? He never told me."

"I'm your taxi."

"Look, Buck, you don't have to—"

"Get in. I'm cold."

The door clapped softly as she settled in the passenger seat. In the glow of his dashboard, he saw her mental debate in her expression.

"A friend can pick up another friend, can't he?"

"Yes, but it's you. Buck. You don't even live here anymore, and my dad has you running his errands. Where's Ben? Or Mama?"

He let the rhetorical questions linger and pulled out of the parking lot. "How was the practice?"

"Tonight was just setup, and it was a disaster. The director quit. Next thing I know, Brandi is shoving the script and clipboard at me and Sam Morris is delivering bales of hay."

In the midst of her annoyance, he caught a hint of pride. "This town is lucky to have you, Jo."

From the speakers, Nat King Cole sang of chestnuts roasting on an open fire.

"Yeah, well, don't skate too often over my good graces." She sighed. "Who am I kidding? I love our Christmas traditions. I'll do whatever is needed. And the kids are sweet. We actually want to expand the theater to spring shows, even summer stock."

"Who's writing the original Christmas song this year? Anyone take over Granny June's job?"

"No one. The last two years I cheated and pulled a song from the eighties, but Brandi warned me not to do it again." She swiveled toward him. "I should. For sticking me with the director job."

"How about I write the song?"

"Buck, no, I wasn't hinting at anything. I was just talking. Your talents exceed what our little play needs. I can do some rhyming. Tree, ribbons, and presents. Star and far. We're good."

He laughed, and when she joined him, he had the first real taste of being home. Moments like these were what his soul craved.

"Tree, ribbon, and presents?"

"I said star and far, give me a break. I write promo copy, not poetry."

"All right, you're coming to the house for dinner tomorrow night. The folks would love to see you. Now that Sadie and her husband moved, there's no one to come for Sunday night dinner. I know Mom misses it. We can work on a song afterward. When do you need it?"

"Tuesday is our first practice. But Buck, please, don't waste your time and talent—"

"So you get to help out the hometown but I don't?"

"I'm not you."

"Meaning?"

"A man who earns millions of dollars for every song he writes."

"You're a snob, Jo. A Hearts Bend snob."

"I beg your pardon. How do you figure?"

"You think you're the only one with time and energy to help? That if someone like me wants to give back, there must be some sort of angle. Or maybe, I don't know, I'll overshadow your efforts?"

"Now you're just talking smack. Okay, fine, wise guy, have it your way. Write the song. But I get final approval."

"Fine." Their voices echoed against the windshield. Buck shot her a side glance. "Did we just argue?"

Her short burst of laughter answered. "What was *that* about?"

"Who knows. We're both tired. Look, Mom would love to help write the song too. She's kind of down with the tumors returning. Songwriting always cheers her up."

"Can we write a song by Tuesday?"

"I wrote '*This One's for You*' in thirty minutes. Cut it and bam, a number-one hit."

"By the way, Buck, I know you do things for Hearts Bend no one knows about. Sorry for accusing you otherwise."

"You didn't. And I don't know what you're talking about, this giving back."

"The new urgent care facility had a mysterious large donation. The elementary school got a new playground, and Rock Mill High's football team has new equipment. Hmm. I wonder..."

"Don't look at me. My parents are as likely as anyone. What about Colette Greer? She's a millionaire many times over. And she married ol' Coach Westbrook. There's—"

Her hand landed on his arm. "In case no one ever says it, thank you."

In that moment, the front seat of his expensive, custom SUV became the Castle family rooftop where Jo knew him. Saw through him.

He cleared his throat, fixed his eyes on the road ahead. "So, dinner tomorrow night?"

"Fine, you win."

He pulled along in front of her house where the front porch was trimmed with colorful lights and hopped out to open Jo's door.

"Thanks for the ride." She patted his arm in a friendly, almost dismissive way but remained planted, breathing the same air. "It was good to catch up. Good night."

Buck stepped aside, wrestling with what he wanted to say. "I've missed you." The words escaped, demanding to be heard.

She glanced back at him. "Yeah, me too."

"Look out, I might climb the tree tonight and tap on your window."

"Well if you do, you'll be staring at the end of Daddy's shotgun." Her laugh sprinkled over him. "He had to cut down the tree by my window. The only one left is by the master bedroom."

"Then we'll have to plant another one."

"Please don't tell me I'll be living here until a sapling grows strong enough for a grown man to climb up to my window. I'll have a granny mustache by then. Night, Buck."

"Until tomorrow. Six o'clock."

She waved and went inside. Buck fell against the side of his car, hands in his pockets, the air fragrant with both the warmth and chill of the coming season.

With no tree to climb, how would he reach Jo? Talk to her? See if what he felt in his heart was real? He couldn't debate it any longer. The moment he saw her in The Wedding Shop he'd fallen in love.

And he wondered what in the world took him so long.

Chapter Four

JOJO

Turned out all Daddy had to do was slap the Datsun engine with a wrench and kick the tires before starting the darn thing without so much as a backfire.

"You flooded the engine, Jo. Be careful."

"I promise you I did not." But it was cold and she'd been eager to get the motor running and heat blasting.

However, halfway to Buck's parents' place, the heater shuddered and died, uttering what might have been a sarcastic *"So long, Jo. Been nice knowing you."*

She banged the dash and moved the heater levers to no avail. This had to be the last straw. Or the next-to-the-last. For sure the next-to-the-next-to-the-last last straw.

As much as she'd love a new car, she was saving her earnings to sweeten her proposition to Haley.

Buy into The Wedding Shop and use her public relations and business skills to build brand and clientele.

Falling in love with gowns and veils, with beaming brides as they glided down the staircase in the perfect dress, had surprised her. She was as dewy- and glassy-eyed as the mothers and grand-mothers.

Turning down the Mathewses' long drive, which always reminded her of the opening scene from *Gone with the Wind*, anticipation surprised her.

Despite all her efforts, thoughts of Buck had pestered her all day. During Sunday worship and the sermon. During a lunch of sandwiches and chips with the family. During her so-called nap, where she mentally inventoried her closet instead of sleeping.

She had *nothing* to wear. Nothing Buck Mathews–nice, anyway. He ran with the bold and beautiful. The smart and sexy. The rich and famous.

Stop, Jo! What did it matter? He was leaving in a few weeks after which she could go back to forgetting him. In the end, she dressed in what was comfortable–jeans and a sweater. She gave some extra effort with her hair and took longer than normal applying her makeup.

JoJo circled her old beater around the drive and parked on the far side of the front stone steps.

The car door creaked in the cold as she stepped out and into the holiday cheer of the Mathews estate. A large antebellum, with three chimneys, perched on the crest of a rolling hill. White lights roped the columns, and every window boasted a glowing wreath.

While she grew up the poorest girl in town, Buck grew up the richest boy. His mother penned the hit "Summertime" when she was only nineteen. Since then it'd been covered by over thirty artists.

In her twenties she married a record label executive and birthed Buck and Sadie, along with more hit songs.

"You coming in?" Buck stood on the front porch, haloed in a warm, beckoning light, his stance reminiscent of a past album cover. "It's cold."

He greeted her on the steps, then walked her in to Owen and Lana Mathews.

"Jo, we live in the same town, but it's been ages." Mrs. Mathews drew her close. "Come into the kitchen. I hope you like Italian. I pulled out my old granny's recipe."

"Add ice cream and I'll be yours for life." Jo greeted Mr. Mathews with a side hug, wondering if she should mention anything about the tumors returning. "Thank y'all for having me."

"We're delighted," Mrs. Mathews said. "Buck told you how I miss my family dinners."

He leaned and whispered over Jo's shoulder, "She's been cooking and singing all afternoon."

"Can I help, Mrs. Mathews?"

"Please, it's Lana and Owen. You're an adult now." She shoved a carton of cherry tomatoes toward her. "You can wash these for the salad."

The atmosphere in the marble and stainless-steel gourmet kitchen was festive with Christmas décor and Jim Reeves singing holiday songs. The island faced the great room, where a million lights and a thousand ornaments dressed a giant balsam fir. A fire danced in the Tennessee limestone fireplace.

Jo felt too much at home. It was both comforting and disconcerting. When she looked up from the tomatoes to see Buck bending over the pot of bubbling sauce, a winged flutter floated through her.

"Jo, Buck said you need the kids' Christmas song. I've been waiting *years* to be asked but never wanted to push out Granny June. Please, can we write it tonight?"

She peered into Lana's tired blue eyes and saw a hunger for hope. How humbling to have this astute, renowned songwriter beg her to write a simple kids' Christmas song.

"We'd be honored to have you write the song."

Her thin hand clasped Jo's. "I'm not going to beat around the bush. I'm sure you know my ordeal. Everyone treats me like I'm so frail, when we don't even know the extent of the tumors yet. Writing gives me hope. Especially for this play, which my children

56

were a part of growing up. I only hope to do as well as Granny June. She so adored it. I'd love to be the new Granny June."

"Mrs. Mathews—Lana—the job is yours." Jo swelled with satisfaction as Lana embraced her.

"Then let's eat so we can get to work. I'm so excited."

Buck stood behind his mother, giving Jo a thumbs-up.

Dinner was lively with lots of catching up and telling stories of growing up in Hearts Bend.

"How do you like working at The Wedding Shop, Jo?" Lana said, still bright with the joy of the songwriting task ahead. "My mother bought her gown from Miss Cora, but the shop was closed by the time I married Owen. I was so glad Sadie could return to the tradition. I think Haley had been open a month when Eric proposed."

"I hope to make it my permanent profession. Lana, this sauce is delicious."

The conversation flowed through town news and the latest on everyone's family while guiltlessly filling their plates with another round of pasta and homemade bread. Finally, Owen shooed them to the music room.

"I'll clean up. Y'all write the best kids' song ever."

Jo fell in step with Buck as Lana led them to the music room down a wide hallway with carved crown molding.

Their hands brushed twice, and Jo tried to play it off, but he glanced down at her every time.

"Buck, you take the guitar. I'll work from the piano," Lana said.

Jo found a chair away from the man starting to consume her entire being and tried to exhale some of her rising affection. He was so easy, too easy, to be around.

Instead, she focused on the amazing music room. She'd been in here a half dozen times growing up, but it seemed grander than before.

As large as her own mother's living room, dining room, and

kitchen combined, the room's walls boasted guitars, banjos, mandolins, and rows of framed photographs of the family with Nashville legends and country music royalty.

"Jo, do you play? You can take the Nord." She pointed to the red keyboard on the forward wall.

"Not unless you want the song to be to the tune of 'Chopsticks.'"

Lana's laugh drew a wink from Buck, which had Jo gripping the arms of the chair to keep from melting and puddling on the floor.

Good grief. It was a simple wink. She really needed to get ahold of herself.

Lana began a soft, simple melody. "I've been thinking on this all day," she said. "We should try for something traditional. Spiritual. Go for the metaphor of children playing the roles of adults, even the Lord, when we all come to Him like children. Get back to the true meaning of Christmas."

"Jo?" Buck said.

"I-I love it. Y'all are the experts." Lana's speaking about Christmas and Jesus changed the atmosphere.

Buck suggested a chord change in his mother's progression, and the two of them began playing, singing extemporaneously, trying out words and rhymes. Then Lana would make notes on a yellow legal pad, and they'd begin again.

Owen carried in an armload of wood and started a fire. "I decided to make homemade ice cream. I know it's cold out, but I wanted something sweet. Jo, you in? I'll bring in bowls when it's done."

"Don't got to all the trouble on my account," she said. "But I love ice cream."

"Jo may never leave, honey."

"Fine with me." Owen nodded in her direction with the most fatherly, accepting smile.

"Fine with me too," Buck said, his gaze intent, too intent, on her. "Mom, what if we try six-eight instead of four-four? Change it up a bit."

This must stop. The hinting and flirting. She wasn't sixteen anymore, hoping he'd ask her to the movies. Did he really intend to stay in Hearts Bend? To court her? And what did he mean by echoing, *"Me too"*?

Lana was singing, and her clear voice filled the room. "Christmas star, of heaven's light, come to save us from our plight. A child like me, He knows my name, Son of God, Son of Man. I think we can make *man* rhyme, don't you, Buck?"

"Let's work it. You've hit the comparison of Jesus being like one of the children in the cast." Buck strummed louder and added a tag. "Come, Christmastime, remind us all, of the love we share. Come, Christmastime, remind us all, of the love we share."

Jo sat back, listening, sinking into the sounds and process of creating. The melody, the lyrics seemed simple enough, but there was a weighty hush in the room. An "other than" feeling.

"I love it," Jo whispered.

Lana scribbled lyrics and chords on a yellow legal pad. "Buck?"

He played the song again, concentrating on something Jo couldn't see, adding and changing the cadence of the chorus. "Mom, let's go over the chorus again. Jo, what do you think about..."

For the next hour Buck and his mom sang ideas, words, and lines back and forth. In awe, Jo surprised herself by offering a suggestion.

"What if you changed the chorus? Instead of repeating the line, you could sing, 'Come, Christmastime, remind us all, of His loving care'?"

"Buck, we've been had. She's a lyricist and didn't know it." Lana scribbled the change on her legal pad. "How did we not see this before?"

"Y'all were doing all the heavy lifting. I just heard that one line."

For another thirty minutes they played the song through until at last Buck turned to Jo for the seal of approval.

"I think it'll be the best Christmas song ever," she said.

The trio congratulated one another with hugs—Jo lingered a moment or two in Buck's arms. Why not? She'd never pass this way again.

"Why don't we mull the song over for a day," Lana said. "If we like it in the morning, Buck can lay it down for your Tuesday practice." She handed Jo the legal pad with "*A Christmas Star*" by Lana Mathews, Buck Mathews, and JoJo Castle.

"No, no, I was only moral support. Take my name off."

Buck continued to strum a low, almost haunting melody on his guitar. "You contributed to the tag. In this business we say, 'a third for a word.' A third of the song is yours."

"He's right, Jo. How does it feel? Your first cowrite."

"And my last, I'm sure." She floated on the sound of her own laughter. A much-needed medicine.

"I'm going to see how your dad is coming with the ice cream."

When Lana had gone, Buck motioned for Jo to sit next to him. She hesitated, then did as he bid, her soul soft and willing from the peaceful quiet, from the lingering melodies.

"Your mom never changes," Jo said, slowly settling back against the thick cushion. "She's as lovely as ever."

"Working on this song means the world to her. Thank you, Jo. Makes her feel like she's still a part of life. That the tumors don't define her."

"I don't know why I got all riled about it. I guess I didn't want to bother her. Or you. I know people ask you for stuff all the time. It has to be wearying."

"Maybe you just didn't want to be near me?"

"Why, do you bite?" She enjoyed making him laugh. "We're old friends. It's good to catch up."

Buck set his guitar aside. "Yeah, old friends. Good to catch up."

"I saw you in concert once," she blurted. "Dallas. Right when I moved there. I told my new colleagues we grew up together, and I was the hit of the office."

"You never said anything. I'd have invited you backstage."

"Why didn't you contact *me*? I gather now that you knew I lived there."

He sighed. "I don't know. Some of those early days are a blur. In the beginning, I unconsciously looked for you in the audience and wondered how you thought I was doing. 'Hey Jo,'" he said in a faint voice, calling to the imaginary scenario. "'Isn't this what we dreamed about?' When I realized what I was doing, I told myself to grow up, move on. You certainly had."

"Not as much as you think. And the dreaming was all yours." Their eyes met. "I am proud of you, Buck."

He slipped his arm around her shoulders and pulled her to him. "Are you, Jo? Really? Because I'm starting to think—"

"Ice cream. Who wants ice cream?"

Buck released her and reached for the bowls his daddy offered, passing one to Jo.

"Mmm, smells good." She sank down into the sofa. *Smells good? What kind of response was that?* She blamed Buck. He had her all turned around and twisted inside out. He was going to *kiss* her, and her lips still buzzed with anticipation.

"Smells good?" Owen laughed. "You can smell ice cream, JoJo?"

She flushed. No way to recover, so she went with it. "It's my superpower."

"I assume you're going to the Christmas dance, Jo?" Lana sat in the adjacent chair with a small bowl in the palm of her hand.

"Wouldn't miss it." JoJo worked her spoon through a large scoop of vanilla drizzled with chocolate, trying to find herself again. Buck intended to kiss her! "It's another great Hearts Bend Christmas tradition."

"One of my favorites. Well, that and Christmas Eve Service followed by the Christmas Eve Walk." Owen held up a spoonful of ice cream as he continued to rattle off the town's charming customs.

The four of them reminisced about every Hearts Bend tradition—winter, spring, summer, and fall. And when they'd exhausted the topic and their specific memories, Lana and Owen collected the empty dishes. Once again, Jo was alone with Buck.

"Jo, go to the dance with me," he said.

"No one takes a date. You know that, Buck. Everyone dances with everyone."

"There's no rule against a date. Dad takes Mom. Reed takes Lila."

"But they're married. And they dance with others all night."

"I want you to go with me. We can dance with others. But I want to arrive and depart with you."

"Buck, what are you doing? I mean, you blow into town for the season and flirt with me. At least it feels like flirting—"

She was in his arms, being kissed by his soft, vanilla-and-chocolate-sweetened lips. Jo held her arms stiff at her side until she collapsed into the thick sofa upholstery, unable to think, let alone breathe.

"Jo," he whispered as he raised his head and pulled her closer. Tighter. "I think—"

She couldn't breathe. For real. Not metaphorically. Panic tightened around her and shoved the last bit of air from her lungs. "No. Stop." She wrenched away and stumbled to her feet. The temperature of the room plummeted, and she felt so cold and alone. Dark shadows crept along the edge of her mind. "I-I have to go."

Her heels echoed down the hall, over the marble floor, and through the high, domed foyer. Yanking her coat and bag from the rack by the door, she ran into the night without a thank-you or good night to her hosts. But she *had* to go. To run.

Striding toward her car through the numbing cold, she fished for her keys, gulping the icy air, trying to fill herself. The strength of his arms, the pressure on her chest, the nearness... In an instant that night in the garage haunted her as if it'd happened yesterday.

"Jo, will you wait?" Buck ran around in front of her. "What's wrong? Can we talk?"

"Where are my stupid keys?" She dumped her bag upside down and dropped to one knee as she parsed the scattered contents. It wasn't his fault he held her too tight. Took her back to another man's terrifying touch.

Over her shoulder, a light beamed down from Buck's phone. "Here." He stooped to retrieve her keys. "Jo, talk to me. What happened?"

"Thank you." She took the keys and scooped the items on the driveway into her bag. "I'm fine. Just need to go. It's late. I'm opening the shop for Haley in the morning."

"It's only nine thirty, and the shop doesn't open until ten. I saw the sign." Buck opened her car door when she couldn't seem to work the handle. "We could watch a movie"

That was it. She had to say it. "Buck, what are you doing? Flirting. Kissing me. Fifteen years of friendship and you've never asked me out, let alone kissed me."

"Doesn't mean I didn't want to kiss you."

"What? You wanted... Forget it. That was another lifetime. We're different people now."

She should get into the car. But something—a misguided sense of obligation?—held her there.

"I thought it would mess up our friendship. Jo, have dinner with me tomorrow night."

"I can't. Choir rehearsal for Christmas Eve."

"What about Tuesday?"

"Play practice. Our first one."

"Wednesday."

"I'm closing the shop for Haley."

"What time? We can dine at eight. Eight thirty. Thursday? I'm in Nashville Friday and Saturday for an Opry performance. Hey, do you want to come?"

His questions were a whirlwind. A tornado blowing over a wildfire of feelings.

"Jo?"

"I have to go." She yanked open the car door and dropped behind the wheel, begging God for the Datsun to start. When the engine fired up, she quickly shifted into gear.

But Buck leaned around the door. "Jo, talk to me. This is about more than our friendship and me kissing you for the first time. Did I step out of line? I'm sorry if I assumed too much. I thought you were feeling the same as me."

She shut off the engine and stepped out of the car, and faced him, drawing from the narrow river of anger that flowed through her since she'd realized nothing good and lasting would be allowed to happen to her or the Castle family.

"You just now figured me out when I loved you all through high school and half of college? How I waited for you to look my way, but you never did? Now you drive into town in your luxury black Range Rover after twelve years of being on the road, doing your thing, and decide you want something from or with or for me? I don't buy it. You're tired, feeling sentimental. I refuse to be some stop along the way of you figuring out what's next in your life."

"You're right. I am tired. I am feeling sentimental. I've missed this corny, quaint town. I've missed you." He sighed and turned away from her. "Jo, I think I've always loved you."

"You think? How reassuring. Don't I feel special. Buck, you and I are not the same people we were in high school. We've barely seen each other the last decade. Our lives are on completely different paths."

"Then let's get on the same path. Are you saying your feelings for me are gone? By the way, why didn't you ever tell me how you felt?"

If he was guilty of sentimentality, she was guilty of nostalgia. But now when he touched her, held her like any man would hold the woman he loved, terror reared its ugly head.

"You mean it wasn't obvious? Buck, who sits up all night on a shingled roof with a guy she doesn't like? I wanted *you* to want *me*." JoJo exhaled a bit of emotional steam. The verbal jousting with him collided with her internal fears. Of how a one-time experience was trying to dictate the rest of her life. "Tomorrow morning, you'll wake up and realize the kiss, this conversation, was just an emotional response to the week, the song, seeing your mom so happy."

"Believe you me, I was not thinking of my mom when I kissed you."

"Maybe kissing me was just a curiosity."

"It was a curiosity all right, but I meant that kiss. I meant it when I said I think I love you."

She toward him. "Then figure out how you can say 'I love you' without the word *think*."

BUCK

Tuesday night he gathered his courage and marched into the kids' rehearsal with "A Christmas Star" recorded on a flash drive.

Up front, JoJo and Mitzi Brooks, the mom of Tony who played Gabriel, were organizing the young players on the stage. Parents littered the chairs, some leaning forward to watch, others on their phones. A few on laptops.

They hadn't talked since the Sunday-night debacle. He gave her space. In the meantime, he arranged and recorded the song in the home studio for tonight's practice.

From the moment she left him in the driveway until now,

he'd wrestled with his confession. Did he love her? Why did he say *think*?

"Afternoon, Jo." He approached the stage with care, holding up the jump drive. "Here's the song. One track with me singing to teach the kids the song. Another with just instruments for the night of the play. I added some lead sheets too. I've got some studio time when I go up to Nashville Friday. I'll add strings and horns for the performance version. If you have any problems, let me know."

She took the jump drive he held out. "Thank you."

"Also I submitted the song to our publisher. Never know if someone is looking for an original Christmas song. I kept your name."

"You shouldn't, but I hope some artist finds it and likes it." She turned to go, and he fished for a word to stop her, draw her back.

She spun around to face him. "Buck, I'm sorry. I was rude Sunday night."

"I blindsided you. Came on a bit strong. I'm sorry."

Their soft laughter mingled.

"I was confused and frustrated."

From the stage, Mitzi stared and gawked. Buck waved. "Hello, Mitzi."

"Hey, Buck," she said with a soft, Southern, flirty lilt.

He returned his attention to Jo. "Are you a little scared?"

She faced away. "Maybe. A little. But I'm sorry you figured that out."

"When you pushed away I felt it."

She held up the jump drive. "Thanks for this. I'm sure they're going to love it."

"Be sure to tell them you helped to write it."

"They won't care." Her smile contained her forgiveness.

"We okay?"

"Of course. We're always okay."

"I'll see you, Jo."

"Buck?"

"Yeah?"

She stepped toward him. "I've been thinking. What's one dance? For our friendship. I'll go with you if the invitation is still valid."

"Are you sure?" He held up his hands. "I promise, no touching or caressing."

"I'm sure. But you'll have to touch me to dance with me."

On the stage, Mitzi had lost control of the actors and they were running around the manger, beating one another with stuffed animals.

"I'd better tame the beasts."

"I'll pick you up next Saturday night at seven o'clock. Are you sure you don't want to come up to the Opry this Saturday night?"

"Thanks, but I'm at the shop all day. Haley and Cole are shopping for baby furniture." She motioned to the stage again. "Besides, we can't have *two* Saturday night dates in a row. You might start *thinking* things."

"Jo." He touched her arm before she backed away. "I am *thinking* things. And I don't regret kissing you. Or what I said."

"Why do I hear a 'but' in your tone?"

So, she'd sensed his hesitation. "You're right. I need to work on the *think* thing. Saying 'I love you' without condition."

It's just if he put his heart on the line and she refused him...

With a nod and slight glisten in her eyes, she turned back toward the stage. "Okay, everyone, places. Dylan, get out of the manger. You're too big to play Baby Jesus."

Buck stepped out of the theater into the bright evening twilight where the warm temperatures staved off another cold snap and the promise of a Christmas snow.

❄

With the evening ahead of him and nothing to do—his folks were at their bridge night with friends—Buck grabbed a coffee and scone at Java Jane's, then stopped at The Wedding Shop when he spotted Cole's truck.

The place was closed, but he spotted his friend inside on a ladder changing one of the canned lights.

"I told JoJo I loved her," he said the moment Cole let him in.

"Are you sure? Because I didn't feel an earthquake." Cole climbed the ladder and fixed the cover over the bulb.

"I kissed her too."

"Dude, what got into you?"

"Music. The fire. Dad's ice cream. Jo herself. We were working on the kids' Christmas song and this wild, weird sensation of love consumed me. It was almost overwhelming. Like someone flipped a switch."

"In all the years you've known her, been her friend, you never went after her. You're home a week and suddenly in love, kissing her? She must've freaked."

"Not at first, but then she pushed away, almost like she was scared. Bolted like a jackrabbit"

Cole moved the ladder over to another light. "Do you? Love her? Hand me that bulb there, will you?"

Buck reached for the large light on the fireplace mantel. "I don't know. I think so. She claims it's just sentiment. To her credit, I couldn't seem to eject the word *think*. 'I think I love you.' Cole, did you know she liked me in high school?"

"Not until Haley told me. But I'm sort of obtuse on romance. Where'd you leave things?"

"To say 'I love you' without caveats. When I took the song by the kids' play tonight, she agreed to go to the Christmas dance with me."

"We don't have dates to the Christmas dance."

"Not you too."

Cole finished his chore and motioned for Buck to follow him

up to the mezzanine. He opened the door to a long and rectangular space. He switched on the light, but the brightness still didn't dull the glow of the town falling through the high, round windows.

"What's this room?" Buck said, taking a sip of coffee. The walls were lined with boxes, two chests of drawers, a large wardrobe, a desk, and one really ugly steamer trunk.

"Storage. Inventory. We call it the closet." Cole opened the ladder and climbed toward another burned-out canned light. "So she's going to the dance with you? That's something."

"What do you know about her? I mean her life after college?" Buck rested against the wall, reimagining how Jo had pushed him away, her expression taut and pale.

His gaze drifted toward the far corner in the room and landed on an airy dress with gold light.

"Buck, hey, buddy, can you hand me that light bulb?"

He heard Cole but couldn't move. The glowing, white dress demanded his attention.

"Yo, Buck!"

"Right, sorry." He found the bulb on the desk and handed it up. "Whose dress is that?"

The contractor looked around. "Haley's. What's it doing out?" He pointed to a battered trunk with dry, dull wood and scarred leather straps. "It belongs in there."

Buck glanced between the dress and the trunk. Surely a dress that beautiful didn't belong in the hideous trunk. It demanded to be seen.

"Why does she keep it in the trunk?"

"It's a special one. Has this interesting history. Like over a hundred years. She's pretty protective of it. Wants to hang on to it for our daughter. Did you know we're having a girl?"

"Haley told me."

"We both grew up with brothers, so a girl is pretty special. We're going to name her Emily, after the first woman who wore

69

the dress. She was a real pioneer, a fighter, a woman of justice. All the brides of the dress are in those picture frames."

Buck examined the photos, reading the engraved names. Emily and Daniel. Mary Grace and Thomas. Hillary and Joel. Charlotte and Tim. Haley and Cole.

What was so special about this particular dress? He inspected it from across the room. How could it be over a hundred years old? It looked brand new. Dad had given him Grandpa Mathewses' bomber jacket and it was worn, the fur lining matted and faded. Smelled old and musty. A treasure to be sure but marked by time.

Cole shouldered the ladder and headed out. "You coming?"

"Yeah." Buck fell in step with his friend with one backward glance at the dress.

At once the room enlarged. Light obscured the rest of the inventory and furniture. JoJo appeared in the corner wearing the dress, smiling, and completely stunning. He couldn't move. Or feel the edge of himself.

The vision burst, fading away as quickly as it came, and he was alone on the mezzanine. Cole's voice echoed from some distant place in the shop.

Buck descended the stairs with a sense of hot and cold, wonder and fear. He'd heard of visions before but never experienced one.

His friend met him in the grand salon, munching on a piece of fried chicken. "So, are you going to pursue her?"

Buck glanced back up the staircase. "I've told her I love her, so yes."

"You *think* you love her. Dude, if you're not sure, then apologize and move on. Don't hurt her."

"I am sure. Well, very nearly." Buck sank down to the first step. "Why do you think I never dated her before? She was always the one in the back of my mind as the 'one day' girl. The *one* I'd settle down with when I was ready. I didn't want to drag her along for twelve years while I was building my career, living on tour buses. And I admit there was a small part of me that wanted to play the field while another part of me was scared to death I'd lose her if I waited too long. Or worse, date her, break up, and lose her forever."

"Geez, Mathews, are you trying to live one of your country songs? 'What if I lose the love of my life, and she never comes back to me?'" His high, twanging voice was sour and off-key.

"You're pitiful."

"Me? A-hem, I'm married to a smoking-hot babe with a kid on the way. What have you got?"

Nothing.

"The question you have to ask yourself," Cole said, turning for the kitchen, his chicken leg picked clean, "is if you're ready to settle down." Buck left the stairs and followed. "Are you ready to come off the road? Because you have to know, JoJo Castle loves Hearts Bend. She's a hometown girl. A homebody. She wants the house in the country with a white picket fence, a hobby farm, horses, chickens, goats, and dogs. Kids. PTA. The whole bit. After Dallas, I know she's not going to want a life on the road. Or anything in the public spotlight."

Cole tossed the chicken bone in the trash and washed his hands at the sink.

"Dallas? What happened in Dallas?"

"You don't know? It's why she came home."

"She told me it was because she missed HB. Wanted to be near her parents."

Cole started to speak but refrained with a shake of his head. "It's her story to tell." He glanced at his pinging phone. "Got to run. Meeting a new client for dinner."

Buck walked out with him, giving a passing glance up the grand staircase to the mezzanine, his heart thudding at the image of JoJo in the white, "glowing" dress.

He fell a little bit more in love. But he had work to do. Besides saying "I love you," without the word *think*. He had to discover what happened in Dallas.

Chapter Five

JoJo

"And there he was, kissing me." She jerked a gown over a white, headless mannequin.

"Easy, the dress didn't do anything to you." Haley reached to steady the fake bride. "You know he was here last night talking to Cole about you."

"Really? What did he say?"

Haley recounted Cole's version of Buck's story. And it sounded like the one Jo knew. The one about the kiss and the *thinks*.

"I can't believe he talked to Cole about me."

"Why not? You're talking to me about him. Jo, it's Buck Mathews. Your Buck. The one you've loved since ninth grade."

"He's not my Buck. And I didn't love him. Just liked him a lot. Besides, he was different then."

"You mean not a superstar." When the bells on the door clattered, Haley walked over to the mezzanine railing. "Afternoon, Mr. Drew. Just leave the mail on the counter."

"How can his fame and fortune not change him? Change his

perspective?" JoJo hoisted the fiberglass form and started down to the grand salon. The new gown from Bray-Lindsay was another upgrade for the shop, a bit more on the ritzy side.

JoJo had suggested displaying the gown under the beautiful Christmas lights instead of waiting for spring.

"Some girl will get engaged this season and want to go shopping right away."

"You're getting good at this bridal shop business."

All part of the plan.

"So you didn't like the kiss but you liked the song?" Haley followed Jo with a pair of white gloves.

"Who said I didn't like the kiss?" Jo set the mannequin between the window and the tree. "I loved the song. It's beautiful. I gave them one line, and they gave me a third of the credit. 'A third for a word,' Buck said."

"One word, one kiss, and you're joining the family business." Haley slipped the first glove on one of the posed hands. "What do you think? Too much? But the sleeves are short, so I think it works."

"Try the fingerless lace instead. More elegant. And I'm not joining the family business."

"If you ask me," Haley said over the rhythm of her heels striking the hardwood, "he kissed you for no reason."

"I'm not asking you." She angled forward a bit to see the glove Haley held up. "Yes, that one. The design matches the bodice. He kissed me because he's lonely and nostalgic."

"Oh, please," Haley scoffed as she handed one glove to JoJo. "I've learned a lot about men since I married, and he kissed you for no reason."

"What world are you living in? Men kiss women all the time for no reason."

"Not girls like you."

"What is that supposed to mean?" She slid the glove over the poised hand. *Girls like her.* Was she special? The kind of girl a guy treated differently? Not in her experience. "What do you think? I like it."

Haley stood back to inspect before nodding her approval. "Me too. And Buck kissed you because you're a woman of substance. The kind a man wants to take home to his mother. How convenient you were already at his mother's house."

"You make me sound like a good set of tires. And I was only at his folks' place for the song. That's all. Turns out Lana has wanted to write the town Christmas tune for years." JoJo sank into the gold upholstered chair, reminiscent of Hollywood's regency era.

"We can talk all day about what Buck feels," Haley said. "But neither of us knows for sure since he's not here. The real question is how do you feel?"

"I feel..." A tear escaped the corner of her eye. "Like I've been asleep for a long time and his kiss finally woke me up. But Haley, it terrified me. He wrapped me in his arms, and I felt trapped. I had to get out of there."

"Oh, Jo." Haley knelt beside her. "Did you tell him?"

"No, I can't. He'll see me as a victim, and I couldn't bear it. The more I think of it, the more I realize we can't be a couple. Don't you see, Haley? He belongs to the world. I belong here, in Hearts Bend. My attempt to live outside this cocoon ended horribly."

"Jo, you *were* a victim and a victor. You did something about it. Please, don't let one incident, one creep, rob your confidence or your freedom one more day."

"I tell myself that every time the tension starts to rise. Usually out of nowhere. Yet somehow, I can't shake it. The very idea of leaving Hearts Bend causes an unsettling sensation. Like I'll never totally be at peace again. Even in my own hometown. I'm twenty-nine and live under a cloud of fear. I used to see myself as a kick-butt-and-take-names kind of girl, but now I'm a scared-of-my-shadow girl."

"So what are you going to do about it?"

"Keep walking forward one day at a time. One step at a time. Keep building my life here." JoJo squeezed Haley's hand and drew a deep breath. "I was going to talk to you about this when I had more money, but I want to buy in here with you. If you'll let me."

"Well, well." Haley pulled another chair around to sit. "Cole and I were talking last night about asking you to buy in. If you didn't have enough money, we'd loan it to you or work out some sort of payment plan. Cole's business has really taken off, and I want to be home more when the baby comes. Jo, do you *really* want to own the shop with me?" Haley's eyes glistened. "Because I'd love you to take Tammy's place. She and I were supposed to do this together. I was well into the remodel when Cole told me she never intended to open the shop. She wanted to be a lawyer."

"Really? Because if you mean it, I'm in." The tears and hugs rooted JoJo all the more into the truth she was meant for a small, quiet life in Hearts Bend. She'd found her milieu. "I'll take care of everything when you have the baby even though I still have a lot to learn."

"Don't kid yourself. You've been at this almost as long as me. You're good, Jo. You have ideas, vision. I'm more of the numbers, day-to-day girl." Haley stood, squared her shoulders, and stuck out her hand. "Partners?"

Jo slapped her hand into her cousin's. "Partners."

"Don't look now, Jo," Haley said. "But something really good just happened this Christmas. Not a disaster."

Jo made a face. "It's only the first week of December, so we'll see."

"You're too much." Haley spread her arms wide. "Let go, Jo. Replace all your fears with love."

The shop was busy all morning, and they'd just hit the afternoon lull when Cole's voice boomed through the back door.

Jo looked up as Haley met her husband in the narrow hall between the staircase and grand salon. "What's wrong?"

"Are you all right?"

"Don't I look all right?"

"Judy Denton called Mom. Said the shop was closed. She was all excited because she thought you were having the baby." Cole walked to the front door and turned the Closed sign to Open. "Since it's afternoon I thought something had happened. Maybe you'd gone into early labor." He patted his wife's round belly. "But I guess not."

"Babe, you're the first one I call if I'm in labor." Haley pointed to the dress in the window. "Jo and I were setting up the dress and talking. The customers started coming in and we forgot about the sign. Didn't Judy see people inside?"

Cole, with his disheveled dark hair and flushed cheeks, kissed his wife. "I'm back to work. Jo, Buck seems sincere. You know you love him."

"Don't you have a hammer to swing? And not a word to my dad. Or Ben."

"Too late." Cole's eyes sparkled as he covered his mouth with a fist.

"Is everything all right?" Buck burst through the front door. "The ladies at the coffee shop said Haley had gone into labor."

"Oh good grief. The hazards of a small town." Haley turned to Jo. "Post something on Instagram. Let people know I'm all right."

"I'll do one better." Cole elbowed around Buck and drew his wife outside. Head back, hands cupped around his mouth, he hollered, "Haley is fine. The baby is fine. Spread the word."

A car horn answered, followed by a distant voice down the street. "What are you, the town crier?"

"Only in Hearts Bend," Jo said, watching from the window, arms folded.

"But you love it." Buck stood next to her. "How'd play practice go last night?"

"Very well. They weren't crazy about the song, but the parents loved it."

"Should we write another one?"

"No. The kids will like it by the end. Their parents will regale them with tales of how their Christmas song was written by the great Lana and Buck Mathews."

"Don't forget JoJo Castle." His wink tickled her backbone.

"Makes me feel like a fraud to hear my name as a cowriter." She turned back to the shop's interior with a side glance at Buck.

He wore jeans and an old bomber jacket, his blond hair clean and loose over his clear blue eyes.

"Mom's still talking about the song," he said. "Caught her humming it this morning."

"I remembered her in my prayers."

"It's this time of year that makes me believe in miracles. As for you and me—" Buck reached for her hand just as the shop door opened and Mayor Maynard stepped in.

"Goodness," Jo said. "We've never had so many men darken our door. Mayor, how can I help?"

"Those two." He motioned to Cole and Haley. "Cute kids. Yelling to everyone the baby is fine. But you." He pointed to Jo. "I've been looking all over for you. The town council needs you. Young, fresh mind with modern ideas."

"Me?" She glanced at Buck, who approved with a slow nod. "If you think I can be of help, of course."

"You know Simon Hardy passed on, leaving his place on the council vacant. He lived a good life. Saw HB through some turbulent years. Even when he was ninety-eight years young he still walked three miles every day, never missed church or a council meeting. Then one day, he kept walking straight up to heaven."

The mayor gripped the lapels of his coat and rocked back on his heels, settling in for a good Hearts Bend yarn. He claimed his gift of story was how he got elected.

"I just talked them other guys and gals into the ground."

"Anyhoo, he'd been on the council since the Battle of Nashville. Not really, but you know what I mean. For sure since Eisenhower's first term. We should hold a special election for his seat, but the bylaws say we can select a replacement with the town manager's approval. And well, we've picked you. What do you say? Come shake us up with your social media know-how and ideas on the world. We're about to launch a new tourism campaign, and your public relations experience will be a big help. Plus, the Castles are an ancient Hearts Bend family. Since the turn of the last century. Don't hurt none that you're a might prettier than Simon. I suppose I shouldn't have said that. My apologies."

"It's all right. And thank you. But you really want me?" She wasn't sure she wanted to use her public relations power to draw attention to Hearts Bend. They attracted more than enough tourism and attention being in Nashville's shadow.

"We do. What do you say? Buck Mathews, how the heck are you? I thought you'd forgotten all about us." The mayor clapped his hand into Buck's. "Tell this girl, er, woman, to join the council. We need her."

"I'm sure Jo can make up her own mind."

JoJo regarded Buck. There was something in his tone, in his shifting gaze. Pride mixed with hesitation.

Jo offered her hand to the mayor. "I'll do it. I'd be honored. When's the first meeting?"

"Well how-do and hot dog." The mayor pumped her hand up and down. "I'm thrilled, just thrilled. We all wanted you. Not a dissention among us." He elbowed Buck with a guttural laugh. "Can't say that's ever happened before. Jo, we meet the first and third Monday nights at six. Tina usually caters a nice Ella's Diner meal for us. If we have no urgent business, we enjoy good fellowship. My office will be in touch."

When he'd gone, Jo turned to Buck. "What was that look? When you said I can make up my own mind?"

"No look. Just stating the facts."

"Do you *object* to me being on the town council?"

"Why would I object? I think you'll make a great councilwoman."

"There you go *thinking* again."

"All right, you *will* be a great councilwoman."

The terse exchange dampened the thrill of being invited onto the council.

Haley returned with Cole, shivering, her cheeks pink and nose red. "What did the mayor want?"

"He asked me to be on the town council."

"I hope you said yes," Cole said. "We need a young vibe in that dusty old room. Babe, I need to go. See you at home." He kissed his wife and headed out. "And, Jo, congrats on joining the shop. We'll talk in the New Year."

"You're joining the shop?" Buck said.

"Buying in." She regarded Haley. *Yes?* "I guess we just decided."

He nodded and took a step toward the door. "You're finding your path. Good for you. I need to go too. My manager wants to tell me something face-to-face. Can't imagine what he's cooked up." When he hesitated to move again, Haley made an excuse and dashed up to the mezzanine.

"Jo, I meant what I said."

"About making up my own mind?"

"Yes and about loving you."

"Ah, that you *think* you love me?"

"Do you *think* you love me?"

"I don't know, Buck. Like I said, you ride into town in your black Range Rover and—"

"Fall in love with you?"

"There. That. Stop. It's too much. Too fast. Don't you have a meeting?"

He glanced at his fancy smart watch. "I don't like how we keep ending on a tense note."

"Not true. The last time I said I'd go to the dance with you."

His smile was electric. The power of his "it" factor. "Then I'll see you around, rooftop girl."

"See you around, singing cowboy."

She moved to the window, watching him go.

She was fulfilling her dreams now. The mayor's invitation proved what she'd known all along. Coming home set her on course. Gave her purpose. And she had no desire to leave.

She'd enjoy the holiday dance with Buck then let him know he should move on. *They* were not meant to be.

BUCK

She rattled him. Made him agitated. Answered his questions with questions. He changed lanes on a crowded Nashville interstate, blasted his horn at a rude driver. Jo was becoming more and more a part of Hearts Bend. Shop owner. Town council member.

How would he ever get her to marry him and go on the road? Marry him? His thought surprised him. He'd moved from love to marriage in one giant step.

Maybe he read the situation all wrong. Maybe they weren't meant to be together. They were on different paths. But he'd said it. The *love* word. At least he thought he loved her.

His laugh echoed against the windshield. Being an award-winning country singer didn't make him immune to romantic insecurities. He was terrified JoJo Castle would reject him.

The secret of Dallas remained. Something that made her anxious and scared.

Arriving on Music Row, he parked in the small lot behind Stokes's office and headed inside, humming Dean Martin's version of "*Baby, It's Cold Outside.*"

Stokes waited for him at the door. "Merry Christmas and *you* are welcome."

"What's going on?"

"Come on in. Sit, sit. How was the drive up? My wife said traffic was horrendous." Stokes moved around to his side of the desk and dropped into his chair with a contented sigh, all the while sporting a shark-eating grin. "What's the one goal on your career bucket list we've not been able to achieve?"

"Entertainer of the Year?" He'd been nominated three times but so far never carried away the trophy.

"Okay, two things, but this one will get you the other. Hold on to your hat, Buck."

"I'm not wearing a hat."

"Work with me. You're touring Europe. Don called. Tank Travis backed out, and the promoters want you. You heard me." Stokes jiggled his mouse and then read from his computer screen. "Dublin, Edinburgh, London, Paris, Rome, Berlin, Vienna. And we're just getting started."

"What? Why?" Taking country music to Europe was not an easy task. Only the crème de la crème were invited over the pond. "Does Tank know something we don't?"

Why would promoters ask for Buck Mathews? Tank's thirty-year career recently eclipsed Merle Haggard's. In the nineties, he made world headlines when the Queen asked for a private audience.

Buck ran his palms together and shifted in his seat. His mouth was dry and his pulse erratic. Europe. This was huge. Gigantic.

"There's nothing to know. Tank's youngest daughter got engaged and decided to get married on her grandparents' wedding anniversary. It falls in the middle of the tour. Tank said he'd rather walk his girl down the aisle than tour Europe. He's been enough times anyway. Buck, they asked for you."

"Me?"

"Is there an echo in here? Yes, you. Buck, you're touring Europe. Your first date is in February, so we have a lot to do to get ready. But the timing is perfect. Your new single will drop while we're on the road. We can do a live event showing your European fans going nuts over it." Stokes popped his hands together. "You're going to the moon, man. To the moon. I'm working to get you home for a month before the American tour starts. The year will be busy, so I guess it's serendipitous you took this month off."

"All right, be honest. Who'd they ask before me? Am I like number ten on their list? Will we be in cheap motels? Youth hostels?"

"Who do you think you're talking to, Buck? This is first class all the way. You were number one on every promoter's list. You've made a name over there. So are you in? Rhetorical question, but I have to ask."

Buck fired to his feet. "Yes, holy cow, yes. I'm in. Wow. Merry Christmas to me." He clapped hands with Stokes. "And happy New Year." He sobered quickly. "Okay, let's talk about the band."

They spent the afternoon designing the band, the show, much of which was in place due to his constant touring.

Then they called their top musicians, and every last one of them gave a resounding yes.

"I can't believe we got Cassie Campbell on bass. She's so busy with other bands. But she's the best."

By the time he left the office, his confidence was on fire. With this milestone why not really shoot for the moon? Win JoJo Castle's heart and take her to Europe with him. As his wife.

In his car, his adrenaline faded as the edge of reality crept in. Next year was going to be a lot of hard work. And winning JoJo would not be easy. He had to bring his A-plus game.

First thing? Start saying "I love you" without the conditional *think*.

Leaving Music Row, he headed to his downtown loft for more clothes before going home to Hearts Bend. Then he called Simon Fonda, a friend and world-class jeweler.

"Got a second for me to stop by?"

"We're sitting down to dinner. Join us."

"If there's enough, thanks."

"Need me for anything special?"

"We'll talk when I'm there."

First litmus test on his love. He'd ask Simon to show him designs. Find out how long it'd take to design a custom engagement ring.

If he didn't panic about opening his heart all the way to Jo, then he'd proceed. Carefully. Jo spooked easily. She wasn't like the other women in his circle who liked fine wine and jewels.

Jo loved her family and friends, the people of Hearts Bend. The Kids Theater. And maybe, if all went well, she'd love him.

Chapter Six

❧

JoJo

She saw Buck a few times the following week. He took her to lunch at the Fry Hut on Wednesday and stopped by the shop Thursday to see if *they* needed help with anything.

Haley teased her to no end about it. *"Buck and Jo, sitting in a tree..."*

His show at the Opry went well, and she declared the second rehearsal of the kids Christmas play a triumph. The cast finally loved the song.

At Haley's insistence, JoJo made a fuss for the dance. Bought a dress from *the Vintage Closet*. Her stylist Michele squeezed her in for a trim and highlights followed by a mani-pedi.

On Saturday night, Daddy whistled when she came downstairs. "Who's the lucky man?"

"Just Buck. But don't go getting any ideas."

"Look at you." Ben dropped to the easy chair with a plate of Christmas cookies. "Who are you dudded up for?"

"No one. Just the dance."

"Reed," Mama called to Daddy as she came down the hall in her flared red skirt with the white trim, looking like Mrs. Claus. "You'd better get ready. I set out your shirt and slacks. Wear your church shoes. JoJo, mercy, don't you look nice. Daddy said you have a date. Don't tell me it's with Tom Tucker."

"Or Argos Hill," Ben said.

"Seriously, you think the best I can do is Tom Tucker or Argos Hill? They have to be forty if a day."

"Well, you're approaching thirty. Your daddy's six years older than me. Sooner or later—"

Oh my word. "Buck. Buck Mathews. I'm going with Buck. Daddy, don't pretend Cole didn't tell you Buck said he loved me. *Thinks* he loves me."

Mama gasped and looked up from where she folded tissues into her purse. "He what?"

"You heard me. And don't make a fuss, he's just being sentimental."

"I hope you told him you loved him too," Mama said.

"Of course not. Why would I lie to the boy?"

"Oh, please, you've loved him since, when? Senior year?"

"No," Daddy said. "I think it was her sophomore, when he first shimmied up the tree and knocked on her window."

"You knew about that?"

Mama and Daddy exchanged a look and a laugh. "We were smarter than you back then. And I dare say smarter than you now."

"Why didn't you say something?" When the bell rang, JoJo moved to the door. Ben scrambled from his chair, dusting cookie crumbs from his lap. Mama and Daddy stood shoulder to shoulder, facing the door, smiling.

Suddenly JoJo was sixteen again, embarrassed, nervous, excited, meeting her date at the door while the family watched. The doorbell chimed a second time.

"Jo, your boyfriend is here." Ben, in an off-key singsong voice.

"Will you people stand down? Act natural."

Buck stood on the porch in a charcoal gray suit with the white shirt open at the collar. His overcoat of dark suede shouted his success. His wealth.

"You ready?"

"Let me get my bag." Jo left him on the porch for a reason. To avoid the inquisition committee. Ben was famous for asking people, *"How much did that set you back?"*

"Nice Range Rover. How much did that set you back?"

"Is that a gold smartwatch? Shew. How much did that set you back?"

"Don't be rude, Jo. Invite him in. Buck, welcome, welcome." Mama reached out and dragged him over the threshold. "If you're going to be around for a while, you must come to dinner. Sit around and play guitar."

"I'd be honored." Buck kissed Mama's cheek, then shook Daddy's and Ben's hands. "The place looks great."

"Our dream came true. Reed and Ben have been remodeling as we have time and money, but we're about there. The upstairs bathroom needs to be gutted. Listen to me go on. Buck, how are you? My, you've certainly made all of Hearts Bend proud."

"I'm good. Great, actually. Had some exciting news this week." He glanced at Jo. "But lucky me. I'm going to this dance with the prettiest girl in town."

"Well, the competition's not that stiff." Ben returned to the easy chair, where he polished off his last cookie.

JoJo gently swatted the back of his head. He ducked and laughed.

"Reed, we should get going too," Mama said. "Ben, get showered up and in your good duds. Listen to me telling a man of forty-three to get cleaned up. You wear me out. But I have to do it for EmmyLou. I don't know how you turned the head of that sweet girl, but you did."

Well, that started the perfect diversion. Ben arguing how he didn't want to be hitched to EmmyLou. In reality, they all knew he was madly in love with her. But shame over his past of drinking and carousing lingered with him.

JoJo walked down the front walk next to Buck, passing under the halo of Christmas lights, and slipped into his car as he held open her door.

The fragrance of his cologne perfumed the leather interior and a bit of Jo's heart. How could such a simple, clean fragrance make her want to love someone? But it did.

When Buck got inside he turned to her. "I didn't want to say it in front of everyone, but you look beautiful. My heart's pounding."

She turned away from his gaze, so intense and sincere. "You clean up well too." She reached for her seatbelt.

"Jo?"

When she raised her gaze, he was leaning closer. "Can I kiss you?"

She could only nod. Then his slightly parted, soft lips covered hers, and his hand gently slid around her waist.

At first, she didn't kiss him back but after a moment she was unable to resist his taste. His affection.

Then the exchange became more. As if a wind blew over their slight passion. He drew her closer, and her desires refused to stay dormant and dull.

With an inhale, she angled into him and placed her hand on the side of his face. His skin was smooth and soft.

After another deep kiss, he tapped his forehead to hers. "I could do this all night."

"Daddy will knock on your door in a minute and ask what we're doing." Buck's laugh made her laugh too. "Never mind I'm twenty-nine. I turned sixteen again the moment I moved into my old room."

"I'd want to protect you too, if you were mine." Buck brushed aside a strand of her hair. His finger gliding across her skin was intoxicating. "Is it weird living at home after being on your own?"

"No. I was glad to be back, safe and sound." She angled away from Buck and faced forward.

"Safe?"

"You know, safe as in not big-city. We don't have the same troubles. I love being a part of a family, but I have plenty of space. Daddy built me a sitting room in the attic. And I love working with Hal. Love being in a town where everyone knows your name."

A solid knock on Buck's window startled them both. Jo slapped her hand over her heart. "Daddy!"

Buck's window motored down. "We're going, sir."

"See that you do."

Buck turned the key, and the expensive motor hummed. When he glanced at Jo, they filled the car with the echo of their amusement.

"I love your dad."

"Me too."

Buck selected a Christmas playlist and shifted into gear. As the car moved, Jo realized she felt lighter. Freer.

"Look, it's snowing." Buck bent to see the snow falling through the light of the streetlamp. "I heard we were going to have a warm Christmas."

Jo smiled. "I heard we were going to have snow."

The snow provided a romantic ambience to what she hoped would be a perfect evening. Afterwards she'd store her one and only date with Buck Mathews in her memories and go on with her life.

BUCK

When he held JoJo in his arms and danced under the amber lights of the town community center, everything about his public life faded.

His fame. Fortune. European tour. In fact, once he left Stokes's office, he barely thought about the big tour. He'd not even told his parents. It just didn't seem relevant.

"How's your holiday shopping?" Jo said, turning with him in a slow dance.

"Finished. All but one gift. You?"

"Same. All but one."

"Ah, Jo, you don't have to get me anything."

She laughed and swatted at him. "I didn't. Please don't get me a gift either."

"This is my gift," he said, gently holding her close. "You in my arms."

"You'll make me swoon with that sort of talk."

"I'll be here to catch you."

Jo rested against his chest and Buck settled his cheek against her hair. Lyrics and melodies rambled through him, trying to make a song out of the way she made him feel.

"You're humming," she said, lifting her head.

"Am I?" He peered down at her. "I think you're making my heart sing."

"You think?" The spell of her smile shivered down his spine. "There's *that* word again."

"Fine, you are absolutely making my heart sing."

She leaned against him again and everything faded but the feel of her hip beneath his palm and the music.

He didn't want to think about the New Year. The tour. When everything would go back to the usual. Not without JoJo in his life.

Too soon the band took a break, and Buck led her to the chairs along the wall. Mayor Maynard made his way over to them.

"Jo, the council wants to talk about the tourist campaign right after the holidays. We've budgeted well and have some money saved. So bring your ideas. Buck." The mayor clapped him on his shoulder. "Perhaps we could persuade you to sing for us this holiday season. Maybe even do a benefit concert in the spring."

"I'll be touring most of the spring, but I'll see what I can do."

"Touring," Jo said. "Back on the road so soon? You never said."

She almost sounded disappointed. Or was it his imagination?

"I never told you about my trip up to Nashville. To see my agent." He might as well tell her now. The atmosphere and ambience were perfect. He'd wanted to wow her before bringing up Europe and marriage, but well, the way she fit in his arms—

"Stokes had some pretty incredible news when I went to see him." Buck took two punch cups from the cart Rock Smith pushed past them. "I'm touring Europe this spring. Me, Buck Mathews."

Wayne Newton sang "Rockin' Around the Christmas Tree" over the loudspeakers while the band huddled at the food table.

"Europe? Buck, that's amazing. But what about your mom? I thought you wanted to be around for her battle." She sipped the red concoction and waited for him to reply.

"I do. And I will be." Her tone caused a sliver of resentment to press him. Who was she to judge? "Jo, it's Europe. The promoters are asking for me. To replace Tank Travis."

"Well, then, by all means. You have to go." She sipped her punch without meeting his gaze. "You'll be a smash hit. Congratulations."

"I'd say thanks except for your sarcasm. Jo, I'll be around for Mom. I don't leave until February."

"You don't have to explain to me. I'm not your Lord. Your keeper. What did your mother say when you told her?"

"I haven't yet."

"Because?"

"I'll tell them. By the way, I don't like your implication I'm running out on my mother." He stood and paced toward the door then whirled around to her. "I thought you'd be excited. Europe, Jo. The place you always dreamed of seeing. I was thinking—"

A burst of music from the bandstand drew her attention to the dance floor. "We should get back out there. We're breaking tradition by not dancing with everyone."

"Jo, wait." He reached for her but before he could voice his desire for her to go with him, two married friends from high school, Jack and Taylor Forrester, snatched each of them away.

"Come on, Buck, dance with me." Taylor was a photographer and granddaughter of ol' Coach Westbrook. She and her sister operated The Wedding Chapel off River Road.

"You're with me, Jo," Jack said.

A few years ahead of Jo and Buck, he'd had been one of the troubled kids in high school. But he'd fought to shed his chains, married well, and landed on his feet.

Buck didn't dance with Jo the rest of the night. After Taylor it was Mitzi Brooks and Brandi Walsh. Then his mom, followed by Jo's mother. Then Mrs. Maynard and his high school music teacher, wives of friends. Old girlfriends.

All the while, he kept one eye on her. Stunning JoJo. And he wanted her in every way. Coming home, returning to ground, was exactly what he needed. Finding love was a beautiful, unexpected bonus.

But what about Mom? Was he wrong to go to Europe when she might be facing another round of surgery and chemo? She'd been to the doctor for more tests and she all but promised results before Christmas.

At eleven the band retired. Buck squeezed through the spent, yet content, throng of dancers until he found Jo. He refused to end the night without his hand locked with hers.

"Hey," she said.

"Hey back."

At the mike, Reverend Michaels gathered everyone's attention and said a closing prayer. Then the junior high 4-H club passed out candles for the closing song, "*O Holy Night.*"

JoJo's voice blended with Buck's, the candle flame casting a peaceful glow on her glistening face. Despite the tension over their conversation, he sank all the way into love.

No *think* about it.

The song left a reverent quiet in the room, and for a good long minute, no one moved. Then folks shifted and voices began muttering "Good night" and "Merry Christmas."

Buck gathered their coats and led Jo out into the cleansing cold. The snow had continued to fall, and the entire town was a picturesque winter wonderland.

"What a lovely evening." Jo's voice matched the quietness of the snow.

"Good night, Buck," someone said. "Good night, Jo."

"Good night."

The calls echoed through the trees, around the parking lot. At his car, Buck leaned against the passenger door and drew Jo close.

"I don't like the tension between us," he said, his face so very near to hers. A touch of peppermint scented her warm breath.

"Me neither. I'm sorry. It's none of my business if you go to Europe."

"I'd like it to be."

"But it's not." She brushed crystals of snow from his coat lapel. "Thank you for tonight though. I had fun."

"Me too. I don't want it to end. Not so much tonight but us. Being together. I want to be with you, Jo."

She stepped out of his arm and buttoned her coat. As she pulled on her gloves, she stared toward the street.

"I was mugged. In the garage of my apartment complex. That's why I left Dallas."

"What? Jo—" He resisted the urge to reach for her. She seemed to want to tell this story with space between them.

"It's why I came home. I tried to live with it, put it behind me, but everywhere I looked, everywhere I went, I saw someone lurking in the shadows. After it happened, a friend came up behind me at a party, said my name, and I swung around so hard I pushed him over a coffee table."

She paused with a long exhale. Buck waited for her to continue.

"I'd arrived home late from an event. We did a lot of work for the Cowboys and Mavericks, and I was the firm's boots on the ground. I was tagged in all their social media, so I occasionally received weird messages from cyber stalkers."

"Did you tell your firm? They should've looked into those things."

"They did, but in the end, it was nothing. I wasn't afraid. Our office building was secure. I was never alone when I was in public with the teams. My apartment had security in the lobby as well as the garage entrance. I had no qualms whatsoever about crossing the parking garage to the elevator. The garage was well lit. One night I'd just pushed the elevator to my floor when someone grabbed me from behind." She pressed her fingers to her lips. "A man...seemingly out of nowhere...pulled me down by my hair and started kicking me in the ribs."

A soft sob sprinkled her confession, and Buck took her in his arms.

"He called me all sorts of names, blamed me for stuff. Like his own pain. It was crazy. I screamed and screamed but he kept covering my mouth with his filthy hand. I couldn't see him. He wore a mask."

"Jo," Buck whispered.

"Then the scent of bourbon and the man's cologne, Creed Aventus, hit me and I knew instantly my attacker was the guy I'd been seeing. Curt." She freed herself from his embrace.

"What?"

"By now he's shoved me inside the elevator car and tore at my clothes. Every time I said his name, he punched or slapped me. So I kept fighting and kicking, screaming if I had breath. We hadn't been together intimately so it wasn't, you know, as if, well... He told me he loved me then held me so tight every ounce of air left my lungs. I tried to reason with him, asked to talk about what was troubling him. But he covered my mouth with tape. It was like being in a horror film. I kept thinking, 'What a stupid way to die.' Somewhere in there I begged God to help me. I thought Curt was going to seriously harm me when suddenly the doors opened and a bright light flooded in. Curt jumped up and ran out. This man wearing a purple shirt helped me up, removed the tape, and asked me if I was all right." She hesitated, started to say something then shook it away. "Anyway, I tried to thank him but I couldn't move. Couldn't speak. I was so shaken. I couldn't even cry. Next thing I remember was a bright light in the distance as the elevator doors closed."

"Did you see your rescuer again? It's odd you'd remember the color of his shirt."

"No, I never saw him again. Not in Dallas anyway. The color of the shirt was unique, a rich, almost otherworldly color. I'm not sure I've ever seen it before." Jo gazed in the direction of downtown. Of the shop.

"Did you call the police? Tell anyone?"

"I called the police. After talking with them, I wanted to put it behind me. It was Christmastime, and I wanted to enjoy the season with the family. I came home and put it out of my mind. In the New Year, I'd return to work, return to normal. But a year later I was still on edge. Not sleeping. Jittery. Still feel jittery. Don't trust strangers or people I don't know well. I thought I knew Curt. He was well respected in the sportswear community. A good man. Apparently not. I tell myself how blessed I am. That he didn't really hurt me. Not really. He just terrified me. But every Christmas, I feel an edge cutting against my peace, my joy, like I'm bracing for the attack all over again. Then I remember all the Castle family holiday-time disasters. Mama, Daddy, Ben, although he did most of his own harm, and finally me."

"What did the police say?"

"It was Curt's word against mine. I get it. Without any priors, what could they do to convict him? I could've been the angry, bitter girlfriend."

"When I kissed you in the music room—"

"You held me so tight."

"I'm sorry, Jo."

The snow continued to fall as she shared her burden.

"I kept thinking, why me? How did I not know? How was I so fooled? Haley says I'm still living with the fear, and I think she might be right, but I'm not sure I know how to let go."

"Marry me, Jo." The proposal came without presumption or demand. But he had to speak. The question burned in his chest. "I love you, and I promise I'll keep you safe."

"What?"

"Marry me. Please. I love you, and I'll protect you."

"Buck, you can't make that promise. Especially someone in your position."

"I have a security team. They know what they're doing." He patted his pocket for the ring box. "I'd get down on one knee if the snow wasn't so deep. You might have to dive in and rescue me." His airy, shaky laugh was no match for the stiff, cold tension.

"Is that a ring?" Jo pointed to the box in his hand.

"I designed it for you. But if you don't like it—"

"You bought me a ring? Two weeks ago you couldn't say you loved me without thinking about it. Now you have a ring?" She turned away from him then back again. "Buck, no. My life is here. Yours is out there."

"Come with me to Europe. Our first year will be hectic, but I'm settling down next year. I promise. I want to buy a place here. Fix it up. Start a family."

"You'll come off the road just like that? What if the next year another huge opportunity comes along? Are you saying you'd turn it down to putz around Hearts Bend? I can't see it, Buck. It's not you."

"Why not? I can do shows in Nashville, gig around here. Rest. I need rest. I'll work on the house. Make babies with you. Jo, I know this is happening fast, but I love you. Hear that? No *think*. I've probably loved you for a long time. But I wasn't ready. We weren't ready. Will you marry me?"

"I'm buying into the shop. Haley is counting on me. I'm on the town council. I can't just run off for a year. Besides, I don't want a life on the road. I want one here, in my own home with a man who comes home every night."

"I'll be home every *day* and every night when I'm not touring. You'll be sick of me."

"No, Buck, no. What do we really know about each other?" The floodlights of the auditorium shut down, leaving them in shadows. "It's one thing to go with you to the Christmas dance, to reminisce about our youth. But to commit our lives? We've not had any shared experiences since high school."

"But we're good together, Jo. I know you, your family. You ground me, remind me of who I really am. We'll get to know each other in Europe. We'll take time off. See the sights. Squeeze in a honeymoon."

"Squeeze in? How romantic. I don't want a honeymoon on the road with a band and crew, Buck. I appreciate what you're saying, but why does my life have to bend for yours? If you love me, stay here." She raised her chin, her profile a silhouette. "I may not be as famous or as rich as you, but what about my opportunities? The things I love to do?"

"You can't be serious. Give up a European tour for a twice-a-month council meeting and a wedding shop open forty hours a week? Jo, this tour will define my career. Twelve years in the making. Next year, we can focus on the shop and the council."

"Do you hear yourself? Haley's baby will be a year old and the mayor will have replaced me with someone else."

"All right, then marry me next fall. The real question is, do you love me?"

"Buck, you're not supposed to be here messing up my life." When she turned to walk away, she sank into a small drift of snow. Stumbling, she shook the elements from her shoes, her coat. "You can't be in love with me. You can't."

"Jo." Buck walked over to her and gently placed his hands on her shoulders. "I am. When I designed the ring, I never felt more sure of anything in my life." He murmured against her ear, "Will you be my wife?"

"Stop talking. I can't think."

He released her. He'd said enough. Done enough. He was about to invite her into the car when the clear sound of sleigh bells rang through the air.

A horse pulling a cutter stopped beside them.

"Beauty, did they forget you?" JoJo greeted the mare, running her hand down her sleek neck.

"I'm right here, Jo." Bo Williams came out from behind a tree. "I just thought you two might like a midnight ride."

"Old Bo," she said, peeking around the horse at Buck.

"What do you say, Jo? Let's go for a sleigh ride."

"Can I sing 'Jingle Bells'?" An airiness had return to her tone, and her low laugh reflected none of the story she'd just shared.

"If you feel you must." Buck reached for her hand. "Jo, are you all right? If you want to talk—"

"Yes, I'm fine. I'd rather not talk about it. Or marriage."

"Fine." Buck pulled her under Beauty's nose and kissed her. "Will you at least think about it?"

"Come on, get in. Beauty's getting antsy."

He helped her climb under the blanket, then slid in next to her. He was just reaching for the reins when Jo gathered them in her gloved hands and chirruped to Beauty. The mare launched in the direction of Gardenia Park.

"Buck," JoJo said in a low tone, "I can't marry you. But I'm so honored you asked."

"Sorry, I can't hear you. There's a ban on marriage talk during this ride."

"Buck, I'm serious." She looked over at him as Beauty drew the sleigh under the lights of First Avenue. "I want to be honest."

"So do I. Here it is. I'm not giving up. You're worth the wait.

Chapter Seven

JOJO

"This love story gets better and better." Haley's tea mug banged against the shop's checkout counter. "He really proposed?"

"Even had a custom designed ring." Jo spread flyers for the Christmas Eve Walk on the counter, then found the tape to anchor one on the front door glass. "By the way, we are *not* a love story."

"Oh my gosh, oh my gosh. This is really sinking in. Buck asked you to marry him." Haley pressed her hands to her head and spun in a circle, looking for a place to sit in the small salon. Above and around them Elvis sang about a blue Christmas. "How? When? What did you say? Isn't this your dream come true?"

"After the dance. We were standing by his car and the snow falling all around us. We mended a little tiff we'd had during the band's break. Next thing I know I'm telling him about the attack."

"Jo, that's so good. It means you trust him."

"Looking back now, I don't know why I said anything. What's the point? It doesn't change anything."

"It changes everything. You told him your most painful secret willingly. You rejected the shame. Love and trust won."

"How do you make that out? I told him because he's leaving in a few weeks. I won't have to worry about running into him on the street. I don't care if he sees me as a victim."

"Which he doesn't. Jo, why won't you let him love you?" Haley motioned to her hand. "Where's the ring? Was it gorgeous?"

"I didn't even touch the box." Jo snapped a piece of tape from the dispenser and carried a flyer over to the front door glass.

"Why not? Weren't you curious? He made a ring for you."

"Who does that? Makes a custom ring for someone he's only recently reacquainted with after a decade of distance. It's nuts."

"You kill me." Haley greeted entering customers, an older woman with her daughter, or perhaps niece, and invited them to look around.

"We just had to come in. It looked so inviting from the outside."

"As we hoped it would. Please, help yourself to cookies and hot chocolate by the fire." Haley moved toward the young woman. "Do I see a sparkle on your ring finger?"

"Yes, my boyfriend proposed last night."

Jo glanced around as the bride-to-be showed off her ring and introduced herself and her mother. She was beautiful with mocha skin and eyes of love.

Haley pointed them to the Melinda House gowns then stepped back toward Jo. "You should've at least looked at Buck's ring. What if it spoke to you?"

"If it spoke to me I'd go screaming down the street. Hal, I can't marry Buck Mathews because of a ring. You know it has to be beautiful. He has too much money and class for it to be otherwise. There's no point in considering his question. We're different people on different paths."

"So you flat out turned him down?"

"Not flat but in so many words. He's asked me to think about it." Think. There was that word again. "How could he possibly be in love, let alone want to marry me?"

JoJo attached another flyer to the plate glass in the grand salon, then spread the announcements on the table between the gold upholstered chairs.

"Do you love him?" Haley whispered.

"No." What else could Jo say after all her protesting? If she even hinted at the truth, how Buck visited her dreams, or how she thought of him when her soul was quiet, right as she drifted off to sleep or was waking up, Haley would pounce.

The bride called to Haley, so Jo retreated up to the mezzanine. A shipment had arrived and needed to be inventoried.

What did it matter if she loved Buck? She stood solid on the bedrock of one truth. They did not share the same destiny.

But did she? Love Buck Mathews?

He was her best friend in high school even though most of their time together was at night on the rooftop. She could tell him anything and everything. Even girl stuff. And he the same. Telling her stories and truths, fears and desires he told no one else. Even boy stuff.

At one time she considered him her soul mate, but such thoughts were those of an innocent teen looking at a gorgeous boy through the glitter of a pearlescent moonlight.

He did make her laugh. A value she treasured. After the sleigh ride, where she'd accidentally drove the runners up on the sidewalk, she laughed until her sides ached as Buck tried to coax a fed up Beauty back into the street.

"Come on, Beauty. For ol' Buck?" He'd tried to woo her with song, but she tossed her head and snorted.

"She said you're off-key."

"She's the one off-key. Come on, Beauty. Jo, give her a little chirrup."

Jo slapped the reins. *"Get on, Beauty."* The mare bolted, tossing Buck backward into the snow, and trotted all the way back to her man Bo with only Jo in tow.

She'd waited by his SUV, trying not to laugh as he jogged toward her, cold, wet, and all but cursing the horse. On the ride home, he started laughing first and she laughed with him the rest of the way.

Jo retrieved the box cutter from the middle desk drawer and reached for the first package. The box contained a shipment of tulle wedding wraps. She dug the packing information from the bottom of the container and went to the computer to reconcile with the original order.

Her thoughts drifted as she worked. Marriage to Buck? Which Buck, by the way? The man she knew in high school and a few years of college, or the superstar who charmed the world? The Buck who'd been her best friend yet never her love? Or the new Buck who rode into town in his black SUV and fell in love with her? So he claimed.

It just didn't seem possible. She felt as if she'd fallen into some sort of winter wonderland. Surely she'd emerge into the real world soon. At least by the time New Year's revelers finished the first round of "Auld Lang Syne."

But the real issue lay within her. In a place she couldn't quite reach. If she were to love him, how could she have a private life with a public person? How could she shake off her fears?

She preferred to remain hidden. If darkness and harm lurked in her short shadows, what danger dwelled in the long shadows of Buck's fame and fortune cast?

She wanted a family. An old farmhouse with a white picket fence and enough land for a hobby farm. She wanted weekends to ride horses and play games with the children. Host family cookouts in the summer by the pool with the scent of newly mown grass in the air, bake Christmas cookies in a gourmet kitchen, and sit in her husband's arms in the light of the Christmas tree on the eve of the big day, wondering which gift each child would love the most.

With *the* Buck Mathews, her life would be on the road. Probably living in Nashville to be close to the action. Sharing him with the world, with women who found him irresistible and threw their underwear at him during concerts.

Okay, maybe women didn't throw their underwear, but for sure one or two hundred considered it. Never mind the hate that would come at her because she took the sexiest country star off the market. She didn't need the heartache.

What about her aspirations to join The Wedding Shop? Serve on the town council? She'd had several good PR ideas while brushing her teeth just this morning. For the shop and the council.

Jo focused on the order when she heard Haley on the mezzanine.

"She's enamored with the Bray-Lindsay and is coming back tomorrow with her maid of honor. But listen, if you even think you'd want it for your wedding—"

"One more time, Haley." Jo set the packing slip in Haley's accounting basket and turned to the shipment of wraps. "I'm not getting married. These wraps are nice."

Haley didn't even look in the box. "So you're going to tell him no?"

"I'm going to put one of these on the strapless Elnora in the small salon. It adds a nice texture to such a common style."

"You're being ridiculous, Jo. Letting fear win."

"So what if I am?" Jo rose from the desk chair with such force it banged against the wall. "You don't know, Haley. You don't. I know you went to war, but at least in Bagram you knew you had an enemy beyond the base walls. I was mugged by someone I knew, in my own apartment garage, and I live with this ticking tension it could happen again. Something suddenly jumping out and overtaking me."

"I get it but this time the person jumping out and trying to overtake you is Buck. Let love conquer your fear, Jo."

Jo carried the wraps from box to the chest of drawers. "You're seeing what you want, Hal. Even if Dallas never happened, the fact remains Buck and I are not cut from the same cloth. We see life very differently."

Her excuses were stuck on repeat but only because Haley refused to listen.

"I, of all people, applaud your caution. After the mistake I made with Dax, there was no way I trusted myself. Then Cole walked into my life and I realized if I didn't let go and forgive myself, I'd miss out on an amazing man. Jo, the man you've always loved has proposed! What more do you want? A sign in the sky?"

"That would help." She shuffled through the wraps, deciding on one for display. "How *did* you know Cole was the one? If you were so scared and cautious, what changed?"

"The shop was about to open, and I had no inventory except the vintage gowns. None of the dresses I'd ordered had arrived. The only new inventory I had was veils, gloves, garters, hats. I was panicked. Cole drove to Birmingham, slept in his truck, waited for Malone & Co. to open, then begged Charlotte to help me. Which she did."

"And that's how you came to be in possession of *the* wedding dress."

"I was so blown away to see Charlotte, her husband, and assistant parading up the stairs with garment bags and boxes. I fell head over heels right then and there. I knew Cole loved me even if there wasn't anything in it for him." Haley pressed her hand on Jo's arm. "Consider the blessings that will come from being married to Buck. Besides being a hunk of handsome man, he's sweet, kind, and generous. Think how much good you could do with his money and platform. Establish charities and foundations."

"Cole demonstrated his love for you. Buck hasn't done that for me, Hal."

"He proposed, didn't he?"

"He also wants me to go on this last-minute European tour he landed. Tank Travis backed out, and the promoters wanted Buck."

Haley pressed her hand to her forehead. "Cousin, you're killing me. You've always wanted to see Europe."

"Past tense. It doesn't hold the same appeal these days. Besides, I'm buying into the shop and taking over when you have Emily. What about the town council?"

"You can still buy into the shop. Marla can pick up hours. I'll hire another part-timer, and Cole can look over the books and ordering. We can get set before the tour. Before the baby comes. We can make it work. And the town council can wait. Please, you are not going to pause your life for a bimonthly Hearts Bend town council meeting."

"Why is his career so much more important than mine? Do I want to be married to a man who can hold his million-dollar life over my fifty-cent one?"

"I'm sure that's not what he wants, but his opportunity is now. Yours will always be here."

"Haley, can we just drop it? I'm getting a headache. Who's watching the shop?" She couldn't decide on a wrap, so she took several samples to try. "I'm going downstairs."

But as she turned for the door, a beam of light caught her eye. Haley's wedding dress shimmered from the dress form in the corner.

"Haley," Jo whispered, pointing. "Did you get out your wedding dress?"

Haley stepped beside her. "Impossible."

Very. But there it was, swaying and glowing, soaking in the light and casting a swath of ethereal diamonds through the threads across the floor.

"I don't understand." Haley ran her hand up and down her arm as she approached her dress. "How? I hid the trunk key?" She glanced back at Jo. "Did you? If so, tell me, I won't be cross."

"Me? Why would I do it?" JoJo set aside the wraps. "Come on, I'll help you put it away."

Haley opened the trunk as Jo reached for the hem of the ancient and mysterious dress, gently raising it off the form. The material was smooth and silky against her palms. For the life of her, she couldn't explain it, but she felt something like a warm oil on her palms. Her headache eased away, and the tension about marrying Buck Mathews vanished.

BUCK

Tuesday night he sat in the back of the Kids Theater as JoJo praised the players on their final rehearsal, laughing with them at the table along the wall, swilling Kool Aid, and eating cookies.

"Thanks for the song, Mr. Buck." A beautiful little girl with plaits and wide brown eyes dropped her slender, dark arm over his shoulder. "Miss JoJo says it's the best song the Christmas play ever had."

"And Miss JoJo is right about everything, isn't she?"

The girl's eyes popped wide. "My mama says *she's* right about everything."

More of the kids filed past him for the lobby, where their parents waited, and several of them slapped Buck a high five.

When the place emptied, only JoJo remained along with the stage crew. She cleaned up the refreshments without a nod to him. When she finally gave her attention to the back of the auditorium, he stood, offering a single wave. She hesitated, then made her way toward him.

"How long have you been here?" She sat in the chair by the aisle with a sigh, looking weary but very pretty. The shadows in her eyes were not so deep tonight.

"The last hour." He lowered to the seat next to her. "Seems like it went well."

"I'm exhausted. Haley had a doctor's appointment this morning then went to Nashville with Cole for more baby shopping. I closed up and arrived here just as it was time to start." Jo patted the knot of hair on her head, securing it in place.

"Hungry?"

"Starved."

"Buy you dinner?"

"Buck, listen, I think we should—"

The stage lights shut off, leaving the front of the auditorium dark except for a row of track lights and the glow of the Christmas tree in the right corner.

"Jo, we're out. Everything is shut off and locked from here. You got the rest?"

"Yes, thank you, Glen.",

"Buck, good to see you."

"You too." Buck stood again and offered his hand to Jo. "If you're going to tell me we should go our separate ways or something equally depressing, I'm going to need food."

He'd promised himself he'd not give up. She was worth his effort. But Jo's silence since his Saturday night declaration created all sorts of doubts.

He wasn't sure what he expected exactly—a Sunday morning call from a joyful and weeping Jo. *"Yes, I'll marry you."*

Or a Monday morning miracle. *"Buck, I realize how much I want you."*

But she didn't call. So he gathered his courage and made his way over to the Kids Theater.

"I should say no, but I'm tired and hungry." She stood without taking his hand and stepped into the aisle. "But let me be clear. Buck, I can't marry you. I want to make my life here, not on the road. I know you said you would take off the year after next, but that disrupts everything I've accomplished here. I want a small, private life. You... You want everything that comes with fame and fortune."

"I want you."

"How can you? I, I—" She stumbled for her words, so Buck stepped up.

"I've thought about this, Jo. Europe is only three months. You could teleconference in for the town council. Haley's baby isn't due until March or April, right? You could leave the tour early, come home, be there for Haley. For my North American tour, you could join me for a few days at a time. We could pay for extra help at the shop if need be. I'll build in time at home so we'd not be apart more than two weeks."

"You've got this all worked out."

"I'm trying to win you over."

"Win me? Like one of your awards?"

"What? No, Jo, you know what I mean." Winning a woman's love in the real world was nothing like winning awards for the catchy song lyrics he wrote.

"So when would this wedding take place? Next month?" She crossed her arms, waiting, a stern expression making her heart unreadable.

"How about next week?"

She lowered her arms and softened her stance. "Next week?"

"I love you, Jo. I feel like the journey of the past ten, twelve years was leading me to this moment. Being worthy of you."

Tears glistened in her eyes, stirring him with the desire to hold her, reassure her.

"I can't." Her low, weak confession was coated with fear.

"Jo, I'll be with you. Don't let what one man did decide for you. I don't even know him, and he's wrecking my life too."

"Buck, I can't do this now. I'm too tired." She started down the aisle.

"Where are you going?"

"To get my things."

"Okay," Buck said, following her. "You win. I'll give it up. Touring. Recording. The whole bit. We'll have the house and kids, a little farm. I'll be home so much you'll be sick of me. By the way, I told my parents about the tour and they insist I go."

She turned to him with a dubious laugh. "So if they don't

care, why should I? Or they see how valuable this opportunity is so why can't I? I see it, Buck. I do. Go. Set the continent on fire with your brand of country music. But don't quit for me. You'll resent me in the end. Plus, I'd rather not have all of country music down on my head. Not to mention what everyone around town would say. Hearts Bendians are proud of you. Talk about the Castle curse. Making you give up your career? Forget it. Besides, how would you make a living? What would you do for a job? Swing a hammer with Cole? 'Cause I can't be married to a man who doesn't work."

"Write. I've penned a couple of hit songs for artists besides myself. I'd gig around Nashville. Maybe hop over to Memphis or Atlanta."

"You'd never be happy behind the scenes. You can't just be a songwriter, playing at the Bluebird or Tootsie's every now and then. Even if you tried you can't contain your shine, your charisma. You're bound for the Hall of Fame, Buck, and I refuse to get in your way."

"I mean it, Jo. I'll give it up if it means you'll marry me."

"If you give it up, I will never marry you."

"So stay or go, the answer is no?"

When she looked at him, her eyes were dry. Hard. Locked. The shadows flickered past. "Look, if you want to eat, I'm hungry enough to go. But no more marriage talk."

She commanded the conversation. Threw his question to the ground. But he was resolute with his confession. He loved her. What was fame and fortune without it?

"All right, no more marriage talk. Where do you want to eat?"

They decided on Angelo's Pizza as Jo collected her coat and bag from the front row. She switched off the last of the lights as they walked out.

"Meet you there?" Buck said, retrieving his phone to see Stokes was calling. No doubt with more details about the tour.

"See you there."

"I'll wait until I know your car starts." Buck's phone continued to ring.

"Very funny but oh so true."

The Datsun fired up on the first try, and Jo tapped the horn as she headed out of the theater parking lot. It was then the idea hit him. The perfect compromise.

He answered on the last ring, a holy reverence building in his chest. "Stokes, are you sitting down?"

Chapter Eight

※

HALEY

Dinner with Cole was her favorite part of her day. Tonight he'd made his grandmother's beef stew recipe, and the two of them sat by the fire in the glow of the Christmas tree, with large bowls and warm, buttered bread.

"You think Jo will come around?"

"I don't know," she said, stretching out her legs and shifting her body to give the baby some room. "I don't think any of us realized how much the attack affected her."

"If I know Buck, he won't give up easily."

"Did I tell you the dress was out again?"

Cole paused with his bread dunked into the thick stew broth. "How many times is that now?"

"Three."

"Is Marla doing it?"

"I asked her and she said, 'What dress?' Besides, she doesn't have a key to the trunk."

"Charlotte was right. The dress is something special."

A jolt of realization shoved Haley forward. "Oh my word, how did I not see it?"

"See what?"

"The dress. My dress. Charlotte's and Hillary's. Mary Grace's and Emily's."

"It's found its next bride?" he said.

"Jo is the next bride."

"But Buck saw the dress too."

"Even more incredible. We're witnessing a miracle, babe. The dress knew they both needed a push."

Cole laughed. "You don't really think the dress has a mind of its own."

"No, but I think a very Divine Someone is using the dress to have His way. I put the dress away because it was special to me. I didn't want anyone to ruin it. Charlotte put it away because it belonged to her great-grandmother and she considered it part of her inheritance until she realized she had to share its beauty with others. The dress was made to be shared. In fact, when Charlotte passed it on to me, I promised her I'd find the next bride." The more she spoke, the more she understood her responsibility as the caretaker of the dress. "I don't how the dress appears, but I know *why*."

Cole glanced to the ceiling. "Heaven is breaking into our world."

"How do I get Jo to see it?"

"First, get the dress out of the trunk. Maybe something will click if she sees it again and again."

"I married a wise man." Haley leaned over to kiss her husband. "How did I miss the signs? The dress has been in the trunk four years. Buck shows up and suddenly it's escaping and drinking up all the light so you can't ignore it." Haley rubbed her hand over the rising flesh on her arm. "I'm surprised we didn't hear it knocking. 'Let me out. Let me out. I'm too beautiful to be in here.'" She frowned at Cole's laugh. "I'm dead serious, you know."

"I know, and I agree with you. The next bride is Jo. Do you think you can get her to try it on?"

"She fought trying on a veil. A wedding *dress* would be out of the question."

"But you've not asked her to try on this one."

"Okay, I'll do it. I'll leave the rest up to the dress." Haley reclined in her chair and returned to her stew. "How about a Christmas movie? We're behind. *Miracle on 34th Street?*"

After all, weren't miracles at the heart of the season? When God became man to save the world?

All Haley had to do was pass along a wedding dress. Seemed rather simple in comparison.

JOJO

She was just coming out of a meeting with the mayor when she ran into Buck leaning against his dark, sleek Range Rover wearing a backwards ball cap, a black leather jacket, jeans, boots, and a bit of morning scruff on his lean cheeks.

"Just ride in, cowboy?"

"Came in for some whiskey and women," he said, low and gruff, while falling into step with her. "Where you headed, little lady?"

"The li'l ol' wedding shop, but don't go getting any ideas."

"I was thinking you might like to marry me."

Jo stopped with a sigh and faced him, pressing her hand against his arm. "I've faced reality. So should you."

"I'm checking out the Dunwoody house this evening with Keith Niven. Wondered if you'd come. Give me a feminine perspective."

"The Dunwoody house? Really?" The two-story ranch with a touch of mid-century modern was Mama's second favorite house when Jo was growing up. The Scott house being her first. "I didn't know it was for sale."

"Just came on the market."

"What a great place. In the summers, after we went out for ice cream, Mama would ask Daddy to drive by the Dunwoody's."

"Fifteen acres with a pool and barn, space for a garden. Have you ever been inside?"

Jo shook her head. What was he up to with this house business? "You should get your mom to go with you. She'd love to be a part."

"She told me to ask you."

"Buck, you're crossing lines now, and I can't bear to be manipulated."

"Asking you to see a house with me is manipulation?"

"Yes, you're hoping we'll live in it together."

He stepped back as if to give her space. "I'm not manipulating you, Jo. Just trying to cast vision. Let you know I'm serious about coming off the road next year and settling down."

"The house doesn't prove anything except you have the money to spend. Mac Allen owns a house in HB, but he's never here."

"I have family."

"So does he."

"He wasn't born and raised here. Hearts Bend is not his hometown. And what does Mac have to do with me loving you?"

"Did you know Helen Apple has an interior design firm? Ask her to go see the house with you." Helen was a classmate. Former majorette and a scholar.

"But I'm asking you."

She pointed toward the shop. "I have to work. Haley's waiting for me to relieve her. It's her afternoon off. Tell you what. If you buy the house and restore it, I'll be the first to do a cannonball into the pool at your housewarming party."

She'd gone half a dozen steps when he bellowed, "You're just scared, Jo!"

She swung around, fueled with ire. "You think you can bully

a yes out of me?" His arrogance made him seem small, and she resented him for it. "You don't know, Buck, how the attack creeps into my sleep, my subconscious. It's behind me, beside me, *and* in front of me. It could happen again. And then what? Raped? Slashed? Maimed? Killed? Cause next time the guy with the bright light might not be there."

"I'll be there."

"You cannot be everywhere I am."

"Your alternative—hiding—is no safer, Jo. Evil is everywhere. Are you going to live in the ten square miles of downtown Hearts Bend and your father's house for the rest of your life? Don't look now, Jo, but he's *still mugging* you. It's not behind, beside, or in front of you, it's around your neck choking you."

She started toward the shop again. "Call Helen, Buck. She'd love to help you with the house."

By the time she arrived at the shop and stuffed her handbag in the pantry cupboard, she was suffocating with bottled tears.

"Jo?" Haley's voice traveled toward her over the mezzanine railing.

"I'm here." She paused at the bottom of the stairs and peered up at her cousin with a forced smile. "Do you need me to do anything? What are your plans this afternoon? More shopping? Sleep?"

"I might clean out my desk at home. But first, can you give me a hand up here?" Haley said.

She found Haley in the bridal dressing area, her hands clasped in front of her, a weird look on her face.

"I want you to try on something for me."

"Not another veil, please."

"This." Haley stepped aside to reveal *the* wedding gown. The Houdini of wedding dresses. The escape artist. The one with five brides and a century of love stories.

"This isn't funny, Hal."

"I'm not being funny. Please, try it on."

"Did Buck put you up to this? I will not be coerced into something I know is not right for me. Besides, look at it. Won't fit. I'm too tall. And it was made for women of a different era. The waist is like, what, eighteen inches?" In her mind, Jo turned and descended the stairs. But in reality, she remained planted on the landing.

"Humor me."

"Knock, knock. This is where you say, 'Who's there?'"

"I'm serious." Haley implored her with a tender, gentle tone. "For me?"

"I-I can't." The tension of tears filled every part of her. Her eyes burned and watered. Not just from Haley's request or Buck's but from the past five years. "I'd be breaking my rule. I'm not engaged."

"But you want to be, don't you?"

When the first sob broke, she sank to the floor.

Haley curled next to her and cradled Jo's head on her shoulder.

"I don't know why I can't forget, Haley. I'm stuck in that parking garage elevator with a man I thought I could love. I couldn't escape then, and I can't escape now."

Her hard sobs turned to soft weeping. But it was the quaking inside that began to shatter her memories, her fear.

More than Curt's attack. There was the night she sat on the stairs, listening as her father cried alone in a dark living room over the betrayal of good friends.

Mama's sad face when she came home to announce another job loss. Daddy rousting Jo from her bed as flames melted the roof of the trailer. The highway patrolman at the door saying Daddy had been airlifted to the hospital. The Christmas Eve Granny died.

Each time she felt so helpless.

"I'm sorry, Hal. I can't seem to stop."

"Hush, this is healing. And a long time coming." Her cool

hand combed Jo's hair away from her face, and after a moment, Haley offered tender prayers.

When Jo finally sat up and dried her face and reached for the tissues Haley offered, she was trembling and drained.

"So you want me to try on that stupid dress?"

Haley laughed. "You are so much stronger than you know."

Jo pushed off the floor. "Come on. This will be my chance to play the bride since you and Tammy never let me."

"Are you sure?"

"Oh my word, first you beg me, now you're backing down?" Jo stepped behind the divider and peeled off her sweater. "Get the dress."

"This is going to be so fun."

"More like comical."

"I promised Charlotte I'd find the next bride. But I didn't really realize what that meant until the other night. When Buck showed up, so did the dress." Haley slipped the gown over Jo's head. "The best part is the dress won't fit if it's not for you."

"Then you'll shut up about marriage and Buck?" Jo worked her arms through the sleeves, then helped Haley set the bodice.

"Cross my heart. Take off your boots."

As Haley worked the dress buttons, Jo examined the swag drapes of the skirt. Peered at her sock feet peeking out from the V-cut in the hem. The richness of the fabric absorbed the last of her sorrow.

"Can you button it? Or is it too tight?" Jo sucked in her breath, but the bodice needed no extra room. "It has to be too tight."

"Be right back." Haley disappeared and returned a minute later with a pair of shoes and gloves.

"Are those the booties I ordered?"

"You had them sent here, and I hid them. I didn't know why until now."

When Haley had finished buttoning the dress, and Jo the boots, Haley turned her to the mirror.

On first glance, she didn't see herself. Her familiar, shadowed reflection had changed. Instead of a dullness in her eyes, Jo saw a spark. Her complexion was clearer than she remembered. Almost glowing. Her shoulders, once rounded with her burdens, were straight and square.

"I can't believe it fits." Jo smoothed a gloved hand down the glossy white skirt, so simple yet elegant. "It *is* beautiful."

As the words left her lips, the swoosh of a thousand feathers fell over her. The warm oil sensation returned, and the tension she'd always carried dissipated, allowing her to breathe in a deep, pure breath of air.

While her eyes filled with tears, a rumbling laugh sprang out of her.

"What's so funny?" Haley said, smiling.

"The dress..." JoJo fell into her cousin's arms, laughter rolling through her with more intensity than her previous tears. "It fits, Haley. It fits."

The gown with the eighteen-inch waist. The gown that was too short. The gown that was over a hundred years old. The gown without spot or wrinkle.

"I know, I know. But why are you laughing? And, Jo, when I wore the dress, it was a golden ivory. On you it's white as snow."

"I'm free, Hal. I'm free." She twirled in front of the mirror, then patted her chest as if to test it for an echo of fear. "I'm not afraid. I'm not. Truly."

The skirt swished about, then fell into place, the delicate swags draping down from the bodice to make the V at the hem. The pearls at the waist glistened.

"Haley, I can't believe it. I'm free!"

"Jo, you are stunning."

They were hugging, rocking back and forth, laugh-crying, when a voice bellowed from the floor below.

"Hello! Anyone here? I'm looking for JoJo Castle."

Jo leaned over the mezzanine railing. "I'm JoJo. Can I help you?"

"You. You're the reason." The man ran up the steps two at a time. "He's canceled the tour. The biggest opportunity of his career, and mine, I might add, is canceled. We'll never get an opportunity like this again."

"Sir, you're going to have to calm down." Haley stepped between Jo and her accuser. "What's this about?"

"Buck. He's canceled the European tour because he's in love with you." He jammed his long finger at Jo. "Do you know how much this is costing him? Millions. Millions, I tell you."

"He canceled the tour?" Jo glanced at Haley. "To Europe?"

"Listen, you have to talk to him. Tell him to go on the tour. Marry him when he gets back, or say you'll marry him, then break it off. Or marry him now, I don't care. But we need—*he* needs—this tour. It'll take him international!"

"Haley, Buck canceled," Jo said. "For me. He loves me."

"I think you have your romantic grand gesture, Jo."

"I do, don't I?"

"Is anyone listening to me? Did you hear me say *millions?*" The man fussed and paced. "I've talked until I'm out of breath and blue. He's being so stubborn. Buying some broken-down farmhouse that's sure to be a money pit." He wagged his finger at Jo, his dark eyes narrow and angry. "Just to win you over."

"I have to go." Gathering the dress skirt, she ran down the stairs, the white wedding boots kicking at the hem.

"Jo, careful of the dress!"

Out the front door, she ran toward the spot where she'd left Buck standing. He'd be gone by now but she'd find him. Even if she had to run all the way to the Mathewses' spread on Ox Bottom.

"Jo, the church is that way!" someone shouted.

"Have you seen Buck Mathews?"

"In the park."

"Thank you." She paused briefly at Ella's big picture window, scanned the diner for her man just in case—ignoring the penetrating cold—then cut a run for the park.

She was in love with Buck Mathews, and she was no longer afraid.

Chapter Nine

BUCK

Gardenia Park had always been a place of comfort for him. Even though it was smack in the middle of town, he found peace sitting in the cold under the ancient, bare-limbed cottonwoods.

He sat on a bench with a brass plate dedication. "In loving memory of Merle and Hattie Lerner. Sixty-seven years of wedded bliss."

He'd had the ring in his pocket when he met Jo in the street hoping for a Christmas miracle, but she was as closed as ever.

Despite her rejection, he grew confident of his love and affection for her. She was his future. His world outside of music. A place where he was an ordinary man.

After Jo had left him in the street, Keith called. The Dunwoodys were eager and reduced the price again. Buck didn't need to see the house. He already knew it was where he wanted to be.

"Put in a full-price offer."

"Buck, it needs a lot of work."

"I heard some things and know the Dunwoodys need the money more than I do."

He wanted the house to be a blessing to those coming and going. Besides, he loved the old place. So easily saw himself there with JoJo. In fact with all the Castles.

She'd been right about one thing. He came home to be with Mom. How could he take off when she might be facing her toughest health battle?

Stokes's fury pinned Buck's ears back a bit.

"Idiot...career suicide...never get this chance again. You're being a fool. This isn't one of your songs where it all works out in the end."

Maybe the man was right and Buck *was* trying to live out a country ballad. Even his parents disagreed with his choice to cancel.

"Go on the tour. I'll be fine," Mom said.

Buck suddenly saw himself as he was—confused and sitting alone in the park with an expensive, custom-designed engagement ring no one wanted in his pocket.

With a sigh, Buck sat forward, head in his hands. "I wish I'd never come home."

"Buck!"

He didn't raise his head. People had been calling his name all afternoon.

"Buck!"

This time he sat up. The voice sounded adamant.

"Buck!"

"Jo?" He darted around the bench as she ran toward him in a long white gown.

Under the cottonwoods, where the old limbs stretched toward one another like clasping hands, JoJo flew into his arms.

"I will. I will. I'm not afraid anymore." Her arms tightened around his neck. "I was standing on the mezzanine wearing this dress, and the fear was gone. And even if I find I'm still a little scared, so what? I'll have you and love and family and friends.

What can fear really do to me except ruin my life? So I will. If you still want me."

"Jo" He lowered her feet to the ground. "Are you saying you'll marry me?"

"You canceled your tour for me. I can't believe it. Your manager said it was worth millions. *Millions!* Did you really?" Her rushed words were staccato and breathless. "Say something. My heart is beating so fast." She locked her hands with his. "Am I too late? Did I ruin everything by turning you down three times?"

His reply was his kiss. Jo rose to him and surrendered to his passion. The drumming of his pulse rose and fell as their lips broke apart. But only for a breath.

"I love you too, Buck Mathews."

In her eyes, he saw the man he used to be. The man he wanted to be before fame and fortune. Good. Decent. Honest. Kind. And full of faith. A husband and father.

"I want to marry you now, but I'll wait until you're ready," Buck said.

"My darling, I've been ready since before you started kissing me. I'd take you to my bed if I didn't believe a true wedding night mattered, but I do."

"Then when? The spring?" He kissed her again, his hands squeezing her waist and then sliding down her hips.

"Didn't you say something about next week? I want to go with you. On the tour."

He pushed back and gazed into her green eyes. "What about the shop? The town council? I get it, Jo. I do. Your life and career are every bit as important as mine."

"Listen, as your future wife, and the one in charge of our personal finances—"

She made it so easy to laugh. "Job divisions already?"

"I'm good at it, so just make up your mind I'll hold the personal purse strings. We have a house to renovate, and I'd like to contribute to the Kids Theater. And if you don't mind, help

Mama and Daddy. Look, I know it's your money but—"

Her confidence overwhelmed him. "No, babe, it's our money. Yes, yes, and yes. But I have plenty of money. I don't need to go on this tour."

"Of course you do. You haven't achieved all your goals, and I've wanted to see Europe since the first time I heard Julie Andrews sing about music in the hills. I might as well do it with the biggest country music star on the planet."

Buck leaned in and sniffed. "Doesn't smell like you've been drinking."

She shoved him, laughing. "Buck, the most extraordinary thing happened." She glanced down at the wedding dress, and he suddenly realized the woman he saw in his mind's eye that day in the shop stood before him. "Love," she said, "has conquered all my fears."

He kissed her again, eager to taste her freedom. "What about your ownership in the shop? Being on the council?"

"Haley and I will work it out. I actually think Cole would be better for the council now, and I'm going to tell the mayor. Shoot, I'm only twenty-nine. There's plenty of time to be on the council. Or even run for mayor. As for your American tour, I'll split my time between here and the road. I want Cole's company to do the house remodel. Does that work for you?"

She was steamrolling, and he loved it.

"Buck?" She waited, searching his face.

"I'm not sure I heard a word you said. My heart is hammering so loud. But yes, to everything." He lowered to one knee. Never mind the cold, snow-dampened ground. "JoJo Castle, will you marry me?" He pulled the ring box from his pocket and opened the lid.

"Yes, Buck Mathews, I'll marry you."

Her eyes radiated with the moon glow Buck loved so much, and completely whitewashed the last of Jo's sad shadows.

❄

JoJo

Christmas Eve

From the second floor of the Wedding Shop, Jo gazed across First Avenue toward a snow-covered Gardenia Park, where the town work crew had put the finishing touches on her outdoor wedding chapel.

Rays of fading light lingered over the miniature Christmas trees, trimmed in white lights, lining the wide aisle.

Daddy and Uncle Ben had stretched a layer of Visqueen and tar paper over the snow before trimming it with a red runner and the little trees.

The mayor had dispatched the city crew to set up 150 chairs, but from whispers about town, the park and streets would overflow with well-wishers.

By the altar stood two more full-bodied, seven-foot trees, every branch decked with lights, ornaments, and ribbons.

"It's magical, JoJo," Mama said. "I pray it's everything you dreamed."

"Actually, it's nothing I ever imagined. But it's perfect."

After Buck proposed, JoJo went into overdrive. There was the wedding to prepare as well as directing the play and finalizing the Christmas Eve Walk—which took place after the ceremony.

The kids executed a perfect performance two nights ago. The town still whispered about the song. Brandi Walsh was already dropping hints to JoJo about directing next year.

A bootleg recording of the children singing "The Christmas Star" in an otherworldly harmony made it to social media and went semi-viral. Buck's record label was talking about a full-blown Christmas album for next year.

Jordan Walburg played a humble Joseph while little Paylor Perkins glowed as Mary, the mother of Jesus. Baby Austin was a soundly sleeping Jesus.

Lana's doctor thought something was amiss, so he sent her for another scan. Two days ago he called to say not one tumor could be found. The Mathews and Castle families rejoiced together that night.

Christmas simply *was* the most wonderful time of the year. JoJo knew now the Castle family curses had turned to blessings.

"Jo, let's get you in the dress." Haley beckoned her behind the divider.

Despite her run through the streets to the park, the dress remained unstained. Only the boots had needed a good cleaning.

The gown was as rich and silky as the first time she tried it on, and she could not contain her bubbling joy.

"Now this." Haley held up a faux fur bolero. "A lovely accent that doesn't change the heart of the dress."

Next, the faux fur muff trimmed with red roses. At last Haley turned her toward the mirror.

"My most beautiful bride yet."

"Thank you for making me step into this dress. For making me face my fears."

Jo's tears were subtle and sweet and wiped away before ruining her carefully applied mascara. There would be cameras. Lots and lots of cameras. One of JoJo's adjustments to fame. But she was ready. Buck's love made her strong.

Daddy appeared on the mezzanine with a low whistle. "Don't you look like something that walked out of a fancy magazine." He shook his head and lowered his gaze. But not before JoJo caught the sheen in his eyes.

"Don't you start, Daddy, or I'll cry all through the wedding."

He sniffed and wiped his eyes before offering his arm. "Let's get you married. I think the whole town is waiting for you."

"You mean they're waiting for Buck." Which she didn't mind. She was proud of her soon-to-be husband's accomplishments.

"No, I mean *you*."

At the bottom of the stairs, Charlotte Rose and Hillary

Warner, two of the wedding dress's former brides, waited with Haley and Sadie.

Charlotte and Hillary had come from Birmingham on Christmas Eve to escort the next "bride of the dress" down the aisle with Haley and Sadie. To welcome her to their unique club.

"I carried this down the aisle." Hillary handed Jo an embroidered lace handkerchief. "It was my grandmother's."

Charlotte kissed her cheek, then peered into her eyes. "You are the guardian of the dress now. It's up to you to pass it on."

"I'm overwhelmed and honored."

"You'll know what to do when the time is right. He will show you. Just look for a man wearing brilliant purple."

"I've already seen him. Twice. Who is he?"

"A friend of the bride." Charlotte turned JoJo toward the door. "Now relax, have fun. It's your day."

The former brides exited the shop first, making their way across the avenue toward the park. Haley and Sadie followed.

Jo stepped out to see First Avenue, lined with spectators and well-wishers, was guarded by Hearts Bend volunteer mounted police. The horses fell in line with Jo and Daddy as part of the processional.

A stringed quartet began to play "*I Heard the Bells on Christmas Day,*" then changed to "*Silent Night*" as Jo reached the canopied altar where Buck watched, resplendent in his black tux and quivering smile.

The weatherman had predicted a high of thirty-two. A burst of sunlight broke through the final moments of daylight and glinted off the snow.

The guests looked glamorous and regal in their best winter coats, standing as Jo glided by.

For Jo, however, love kept her warm. The cold was far, far away. As she made her way down the aisle between the chairs, she slowed, seeing the man in the purple shirt among the onlookers. Their eyes met, and he nodded. His gaze overflowed with love, and his country superstar smile was only for her.

Nearing his presence, the dress seemed to exhale and fit closer to Jo's body. Yet she could still breathe. She was still free.

She slowed as she passed him. "It's you. From the parking garage. From that day outside the shop."

"From every dark moment, from every trial, every happy moment. I've been here all along."

He was the champion of the dress. Like Charlotte said. The one who would show her what to do. The one who made sure it was always in style, always beautiful, and fit every bride who tried it on.

He was the *one* who chased away her fears.

Daddy gently urged her the rest of the way to the altar. She locked eyes with Buck, and the presence of his love nearly consumed her.

When Daddy placed Jo's hand in Buck's, he leaned close. "Treat her wrong and I will hurt you."

"I believe you will."

Turning toward the altar, Buck leaned to speak to Jo, but his lips quivered, and his words faltered. Jo squeezed his hand.

"I know. I'm so very happy too."

So she was married in the glow of the town's Christmas lights. But it wasn't the man-made electric illumination that conquered her fears. It was the heaven-sent power of love.

Merry Christmas.

Did you miss the beginning of the series?
Enjoy an excerpt from

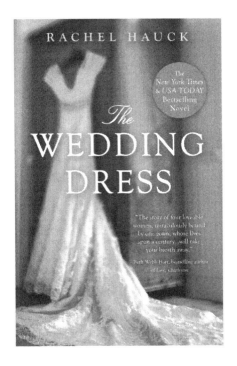

Chapter One

CHARLOTTE

April 14

It was the breeze, a change in the texture of the unseen, that made her look up and walk around a stand of shading beech trees. Charlotte paused on the manicured green of the Ludlow Estate for a pure, deep breath, observing the elements of the day—blue sky, spring trees, sunlight bouncing off the parked-car windshields.

She'd woken up this morning with the need to think, to pray, to get closer to heaven. She'd tugged on her favorite pair of shorts and driven up to the ridge.

But instead of solitude, Charlotte found her piece of Red Mountain busy and burdened with shoppers, seekers and bargain hunters. The annual Ludlow antiques auction to raise money for the poor was in full force on the estate's luscious grounds.

Charlotte raised her sunglasses to the top of her head, resenting the intrusion. This was her personal sanctuary even if the rest of the world didn't know it. Mama used to bring her here for picnics, parking on a gravel service road and sneaking Charlotte along the

Ludlow's perimeter, laughing and whispering, "Shh," as if they were getting away with something fun and juicy.

She'd find a spot on the back side of a knoll, spread a blanket, open a bucket of chicken or a McDonald's bag, and exhale as she looked out over the valley toward the Magic City. "Isn't it beautiful?"

"Yep." Charlotte always said, but her eyes were on Mama, not Birmingham's lights. She was the most beautiful woman Charlotte had ever seen. And almost eighteen years after her death, she still was the most beautiful woman Charlotte had ever seen. Mama had a way of just *being*, but she died before she imparted that gift to Charlotte.

Shouts invaded Charlotte's memorial moment with Mama. Bidders and buyers moved in and out from under the auction tent spread across the side lawn.

Shading her eyes from the angled sunlight, Charlotte stood in the breeze, watching, deciding what to do. Go back home or walk the grounds? She didn't need or want anything that might be under that tent. Didn't have the money to buy even if she did.

What she needed was to think through—pray about—her recent tensions with Tim's family. His sister-in-law Katherine specifically. The whole mess challenged her to reconsider the leap she was about to make.

As Charlotte turned toward her car, the wind bumped her again and she glanced back. Through the trees and beyond the tent, the second-floor windows of the Ludlow stone and glass mansion shone with the golden morning light and appeared to be watching over the proceedings on the ground.

Then the wind shifted the light, a shadow passed over the window and the house seemed to wink at her. *Come and see...*

"Hey there," a lofty woman's voice caused Charlotte to turn around. "You're not leaving already, are you?" She lugged up the slope of the lawn with a box in her hands.

Charlotte recognized her. Not by name or face, but by aura. One of the classic southern woman that populated Birmingham.

Ones with dewy skin, pressed slacks, cotton tops, and a modest string of pearls. She stopped by Charlotte, breathless.

"You've not even gone up to the auction tent. I saw you pull in, sweetie. Now come on, we've beautiful items for auction. Is this your first time here?" She dipped into the box and pulled out a catalog. "Had to run to my car to get more. We're busy, busy this year. Well, you can see that by the cars. Remember now, all the proceeds go to the Ludlow Foundation. We give millions in grants and scholarships around the city."

"I've admired the foundation for quite a while." Charlotte flipped through the catalog.

"I'm Cleo Favorite, president of the Ludlow Foundation." She offered Charlotte her hand. "You're Charlotte Malone."

Charlotte regarded Cleo for a moment, slowly shaking the woman's hand. "Should I be impressed you know me or run screaming back to my car?"

Cleo smiled. Her teeth matched her pearls. "My niece was married last year."

"I see. She bought her dress from my shop?"

"She did, and for a while, I believed she was more excited about working with you than marrying her fiancé. Quite a business you have there."

"I've been very fortunate." More than any poor, orphaned girl dreamed. "Who is your niece?"

"Elizabeth Gunter. She married Dylan Huntington." Cleo started toward the tent. Charlotte followed so as not to be rude.

"Of course, I remember Elizabeth. She was a beautiful bride."

"And she wanted the whole wide world to know it." Cleo laughed with a pop of her hand against the breeze. "She darn-near sent my brother to the poor house. But you only get married once, right?"

"I hear that's the idea." Charlotte touched her thumb to the shank of her engagement ring—the reason she'd driven up here today. She paused at the edge of the tent.

"So, Charlotte, are you looking for any particular item? Something for your shop?" Cleo dropped the box of catalogs on a table and started down the main aisle as if she expected Charlotte would follow. "We have some beautiful wardrobes for sale. The catalog tells you the lot number, when and where to bid. The auctioneer just moves to the piece. We found that to be easier than—well, what does any of that matter? It's a great auction and it runs smoothly. Tell me, what are you looking for?" Cleo tipped her head to one side and clasped her hands together at her waist.

Charlotte stepped under the tent's shade. "Actually, Cleo,"—*I came up here to think*—"my bridal shop is strictly contemporary." Charlotte rolled the catalog in her hand. "But I guess browsing is always fun." She could walk the aisles to think and pray, right?

"Why sure it is. You're bound to find something you like as you...browse." Cleo winked. "It works best if you go ahead and give yourself permission to spend some of your hard-earned money."

"I'll keep that in mind."

Cleo trotted off and Charlotte picked a side aisle to wander, examining the pieces as if the answer she longed for might be lurking among the ancients and the antiques.

Maybe she'd hear, *He's the one,* as she passed a twentieth-century breakfront or a nineteenth-century wardrobe.

But probably not. Answers didn't often just appear to her out of the ethereal realm. Or drop on her suddenly. She worked for her life answers. Just rolled up her sleeves, evaluated the situation, calculated costs, and decided. She'd have never opened Malone & Co. otherwise.

Charlotte paused in front of a dark wood foyer table and traced her fingers over the surface. Gert had one like this in her foyer. Wonder what happened to it? Charlotte bent to see if the underside had been marked with a red magic marker.

It hadn't. Charlotte moved on. That table wasn't Gert's. Oh, she'd been so mad when she discovered her niece had run amuck with that pen.

At the end of the aisle, Charlotte halted with a sigh. She should head back down to the city. Her hair appointment was in a few hours anyway.

Instead, she started down the next aisle, let her thoughts wonder to Tim and the struggle in her heart.

Four months ago she'd been perfectly ensconced in her steady, predictable, comfortable day-to-day life. Then the contractor who remodeled her shop harangued her into accepting his Christmas dinner invitation. He seated her next to Tim Rose and it changed Charlotte's life.

A dull, tired roll top desk caught her eye. Charlotte stopped in front of it and smoothed her hand along the surface. If the grain could talk, what stories would it tell?

Of a husband figuring the family finances? Or of a child working through a homework problem? Of a mama writing a letter to the folks back home?

How many men and women sat at this desk? One or hundreds? What were their hopes and dreams?

One piece of furniture surviving time. Was *that* what she wanted? To survive, to be a part of something important?

She wanted to *feel* like she belonged to the Rose family. Katherine certainly didn't make Charlotte feel like a part of the gregarious collection of siblings, aunts, uncles, cousins, and lifelong friends.

On their first date when Tim told Charlotte he had four brothers, she couldn't even imagine what that felt like. It sounded thrilling. She drilled him with question after question. Charlotte only had Mama. Then old Gert when Mama died.

She'd never lived with a sibling, let alone four of them. Let alone a boy.

Was that why she accepted Tim Rose's proposal after two months? Fascination? At the moment, she wasn't sure her reason was love. She wasn't even sure it was to be part of a big family.

Charlotte glanced down at the one-carat diamond filigree and platinum engagement ring that had belonged to Tim's grandmother.

But the ring had no answers. *She* had no answers.

"Charlotte Malone?" A round, pleasant looking woman approached her from the other side of a dining table. "I read about you in *Southern Weddings*. You look like your picture."

"I hope that's a good thing." Charlotte smiled.

"Oh, it is. Your shop sounds magical. Made me wish I was getting married again."

"We hit a lucky break with that piece." When the editor called last fall, it was the last in a wash of fortunate waves breaking Charlotte's way.

"I've been married thirty-two years and I read *Southern Weddings* about as religiously as the Good Book. I just love weddings, don't you?"

"I certainly love wedding dresses," Charlotte said.

"I suppose you do." The woman's laugh lingered in the air as she said good-bye and moved on, touching Charlotte's arm gently as she passed.

She *did* love wedding dresses. Since she was a girl, the satin and sheen of white gowns practically made her giddy. She loved the way a bride's face changed when she slipped on the perfect gown, the way her hopes and dreams swam in her eyes.

In fact, she was on the verge of her own transformation—slipping on the perfect gown, hopes and dreams swimming in her eyes.

So what was the problem? Why the holdout? She'd considered fifteen dresses, tried on none. June twenty-third would be here before she knew it.

A year ago February, she was barely getting by, investing all her capital in inventory while duct-taping her shop—a 1920's Mountain Brook cottage—together.

Then an anonymous bank check to the tune of a hundred

thousand dollars landed in her account. After weeks of panicked elation trying to find out who would give her so much money, Charlotte redeemed her gift and finally, finally remodeled her shop. And everything changed.

Tawny Boswell, Miss Alabama, became a client and put her on the map. *Southern Weddings* called. Then as if to put a bow on the year, Charlotte attended the Christmas dinner and sat next to a handsome man who charmed everyone in the room. By the time she'd finished her first course of oyster soup, Tim Rose had captured her heart too.

The feathery kiss of destiny sent a shiver over her soul as the breeze rushing over the mountain top tapped her legs. Did she smell rain? Dipping her head to see beyond the lip of the tent, Charlotte saw nothing but the glorious sun possessing a crystal blue sky. Not one vanilla cloud in sight.

She started down the next aisle and her phone buzzed from her jeans pocket. Dixie.

"Hey, Dix, everything okay at the shop?"

"Quiet. But Tawny called. She wants to meet with you tomorrow at three."

Sunday? "Is everything all right? Did she sound okay? Like she was still happy with us?" Charlotte had spent months trying to find the perfect gown for Miss Alabama, lying awake at night, whispering to the God of love to help her fulfill Tawny's dreams.

Then she discovered a new, small designer out of Paris and Charlotte knew she'd found her own brand of white-silk gold. "Call her back and tell her tomorrow is fine. Do we have crackers and cheese in the refreshment bar? Coffee, tea, water, and soda?"

"We're all stocked. Tawny seemed enthusiastic, so I don't think she's going to tell you she's going with another shop."

"How long have we been working in the bridal gown business together, Dix?"

"Five years, ever since you opened this place." Dix, forever pragmatic and calm.

"And how many times have we lost a customer at the last minute?" Even after countless hours of scouring designers to find the perfect gown.

"We didn't know what we were doing then. We're the experts now," Dixie said.

"You know very well it has nothing to do with us. Listen, I'll call Tawny and tell her we'd be happy to see her tomorrow."

"Already told her. Didn't think you'd want to turn her down." Dixie's voice always carried the weight of confidence. She was a godsend. Support beams for Charlotte's dream. "So, where are you anyway, Char?"

"Up on Red Mountain. At the Ludlow estate. I came up here to think but ran into the annual auction crowd. I'm wandering among the antiques as we speak."

"People or things?"

Charlotte grinned, scanning the gray heads among the aisles. "A little of both." She paused in front of a locked glass of jewels. Unique pieces were the perfect accent for her brides. Charlotte maintained an inventory of one-of-a-kind necklaces, earrings, bracelets, and tiaras. It was the small things that helped seal her success.

"Speaking of weddings," Dixie said low and slow.

"Were we?"

"Aren't we always? *Your* wedding invitations are still on the storeroom desk, Charlotte. Do you want me to bring them home tonight?" Dix and her husband Jared, Dr. Hotstuff as she called him, lived in the Homewood loft next door to Charlotte.

"Wait...really? They're still on the storeroom desk? I thought I took them home."

"If you did, they walked back."

"Ha, ha, funny girl you are, Dixie. Yeah, sure, bring them home. I can work on them tomorrow after church. I need to see if Mrs. Rose has a guest list for Tim's side"

"You're meeting with Tawny at three."

"Right, okay, after I meet with her. Or I can work on them Monday night. I don't think I have anything Monday night."

"Charlotte, can I ask you something?"

"No"

"You're getting married in two months and"

"I've just been busy, Dixie, that's all." Charlotte knew where her friend was going with her inquiry. Charlotte had been asking herself the same questions for weeks now and the need for answers drove her up the mountain today. "I've got time."

"But it's running out."

She knew. She knew. "We should've picked a fall wedding date. Fast engagement, fast wedding...it has me spinning."

"Tim is an amazing man, Charlotte."

She knew. She knew. But was he amazing for her? "Listen, I'd better go. I need to get back down the mountain in a few minutes so I can get my hair done. Call you later."

"Have fun tonight, Charlotte. Don't let Katherine get to you. Tell her to bug off. Just *be* there with Tim. Remember why you fell in love in the first place."

"I'll try." Charlotte hung up, Dixie's advice settling in her thoughts. *Remember why you fell in love in the first place.*

It'd all been heart pounding and romantic. She wasn't sure she could identify a real, solid reason out of the whirlwind. As Charlotte made her way down the aisle to leave the tent, she found herself herded toward one side by a gathering crowd.

She smiled at the man beside her and tried to step around him. "Excuse me." He didn't budge, but remained planted, staring pointedly at the item about to be auctioned.

"Pardon me, but if you could let me through, I'll be out of your way. Are you bidding on that" Charlotte looked over her shoulder. "Trunk?" *That ugly trunk?*

"Gather around everybody." The auctioneer jumped on to riser next to the trunk. The crowd of fifteen or twenty surged forward, taking Charlotte with them. She stumbled back, losing her clog in the process. "We're about to start bidding."

Fishing around for her shoe, Charlotte decided to wait it out. The bidders on this item seemed determined. How long could the auction be? Ten minutes? Might be kind of fun to see the whole process up close.

Twenty bucks. The trunk didn't look like it was worth more than that. Charlotte picked around to see who she thought might be willing to shell out money for a dull, battered, and scarred box of wood with frayed and cracked leather straps.

The auctioneer was a man with nothing distinguishable about him. Average height and weight. Hair that might have once been brown but was now...gray? Ash?

Yet he wore a brilliant purple shirt tucked into charcoal gray trousers that he held up with leather suspenders. He bounced on the risers with his very clean and white Nike runners.

Charlotte grinned. She liked him, though when he looked at her, the blue blaze of his eyes made her spirit churn. She took a step back but remained hemmed in on all sides.

"This is lot number zero," the auctioneer said, and his bass voice sank through Charlotte like a warm pearl.

Lot number zero? She fanned the pages of her catalog. There wasn't a lot number zero. She cross-referenced with the itemized listing in the back. But no trunk, or chest, or luggage, or steamer was listed.

"This item was rescued from a house just minutes before it was torn down. The turnk was made in 1912." He leaned over the crowd. "It was made for a bride."

His gaze landed on Charlotte and she jerked back with a gasp. Why was he looking at her? She tucked her ring hand behind her back.

"It's one hundred years old. A century. The hardware and leather are original and the entire piece is in good but thirsty condition."

"What happened to the lock?" The man on Charlotte's left

pointed with his rolled-up catalog to the gnarled brass holding the lid in place.

"Well, that's a tale in and of itself. It got welded shut, you see." The auctioneer leaned farther toward his audience. Again, his roaming, fiery blue eyes stopped on Charlotte. He wiggled his bushy gray eyebrows. "By a gal with a broken heart."

The women in the group "Ooo'd" and angled for a better look at the trunk while Charlotte took another step back. Why was he directing his attention toward her? She pressed her hand against the heat crackling between her ribs.

"But to the one willing, there's great treasure inside."

He scanned the crowd that seemed to grow thicker and winked. Laughter peppered the air and the auctioneer seemed satisfied he'd drawn everyone in.

Okay, Charlotte got it. There wasn't *really* a great treasure inside. He just wanted them to believe there could be. He was quite the salesman. Kudos.

"Let's start the bidding at five," he said.

Several from the crowd peeled away, releasing the pressure Charlotte felt to stay penned in. The swirl of cool air around her legs felt good.

"Do I have five?" he said again.

Charlotte checked the faces of those who remained. Come on, someone, bid five dollars. Now that the trunk had a price and had endured laughter, her sympathies were aroused. Hearing a bit of its story changed its dismal appearance.

Everyone, *everything*, needed love.

Another few seconds ticked by. Bid someone, please. "I'll bid five." Charlotte raised her rolled catalog. She could donate the trunk to the children's ministry at church. They were always looking for items to store toys or to pack with mission trip necessities.

"I have five hundred." The seller held up his hand, wiggling his fingers. "Do I have five-fifty?"

"Five hundred?" She balked. "No, no, I bid five dollars."

"But the price was five hundred." The auctioneer nodded at her. "Always consider the cost, little lady. Now you know the price. Do I have five-fifty?"

Please, someone, bid five-fifty. How could she have been so stupid? The innocent old man routine fooled her.

The man next to Charlotte raised his catalog. "I'll go five-fifty."

Charlotte exhaled, pressing her hand to her chest. Thank you, kind sir. She flipped through the catalog pages again, searching for a description, some information, anything on the trunk. But it was flat not listed.

"Five-fifty, do I have six? Six hundred dollars." The auctioneer's eyes were animated, speaking, and his cheeks glistened red even though the mountain air under the tent was warm for April.

The woman next to Charlotte raised her hand. "Six."

Three more bidders peeled away. Charlotte regarded the trunk through narrow slits, thinking she should just take this time to be on her way, too. She'd experienced enough of the bidding process.

Besides, she wanted to grab a bite of lunch before her appointment. By the time she left the salon, she'd have just time enough to go home and change before Tim picked her up at six.

"Six, do I have six-fifty?" The auctioneer's voice bobbed with each syllable.

"Six-fifty." The man on her left. "I can use it for replacement parts on a steamer I'm restoring."

"Seven hundred," Charlotte said, the words bursting from her lips. She cleared her throat and faced the auctioneer. Used for parts? Never. Something inside her rebelled at the thought of tearing the trunk apart. "This trunk deserves its own tender, loving care."

"That it does, young lady. I rescued it myself. And what I rescue is never destroyed." The auctioneer's eyes radiated blue with each word and sent a burning chill through Charlotte. "Do I have seven-fifty?"

The woman next to her lifted her hand.

"Eight." Charlotte didn't even wait for him to up the bid. "Hundred. Eight hundred."

Run! Get out of here! Charlotte tried to turn but her legs refused to move and her feet remained planted on the Ludlow lawn. A blunt brush of the April breeze cooled the flash of perspiration on her forehead.

She didn't want this trunk. She didn't need this trunk. Her loft was contemporary, small, and so far, clutter free. The way she liked it.

Malone & Co. was an upscale, classy, exquisitely contemporary boutique. Where would she put a beat-up old trunk? Never mind that she'd spent her windfall money on the remodel. Every last dime. And her personal bank account had just enough to foot the expense of a small wedding. Eight hundred dollars for a trunk was not in the budget. If she was going to blow that much cash, she'd buy a pair of Christian Louboutin shoes.

"It calls to you doesn't it?" The man-in-purple leaned toward Charlotte with a swoosh up of his bushy brows.

"Unfortunately, yes." Tim would have a fit if she brought that thing home.

Charlotte regarded the trunk. Who was the man or woman who owned the trunk in days gone by? What about the bride the auctioneer spoke of from 1912—wouldn't she want a home for this battered, old piece?

"Eight-fifty." The second man on Charlotte's left made a bid.

"One thousand dollars." Charlotte clapped her hand over her mouth. But it was too late. She'd made the bid.

Oh, she'd have to explain this to Tim.

"Sold." The auctioneer smacked his palms together and pulled a slip of paper out of his pocket. "This trunk belongs to you."

Charlotte read the pre-printed slip. *Redeemed. $1000.* She whirled around. "Wait, sir, excuse me, but how did you know..."

But he was gone. Along with the crowd and the hum of voices. Charlotte stood completely alone except for the battered trunk and the glittering swirl in the air.

The Wedding Dress is available in ebook and print from your favorite bookstores and online retailers.

Acknowledgments for
The Wedding Dress Christmas

Thank you to...

Erin Healy for your wise edits. You are so good at what you do.

Barbara Curtis for your magical touch.

Lisa Jordan, Annette Irby, and Jen Fitch for giving the story a final read and checking for those nasty typos. But I'm sure we left a few for reader-entertainment.

Kristen Ingebretson for the amazing cover design.

Susan May Warren for sounding out ideas with me and for seventeen years of friendship and partnership. For holding my hand through this process.

My husband for running with me on this crazy writing journey and never batting an eye when I say, "The Lord told me to..." It usually costs us money at the start. I love you.

My mom who cheers me on. Love you, Mom.

Kristen Painter and Leigh Duncan for the lunch in which you challenged me with new ideas.

Amy Atwell for your hard work on this book, and for being so kind and gracious!

To all the readers who write me and tell me how a story has impacted them. I am honored and blown away by the things God does with my simple, humble words. God bless you all.

Merry Christmas!

About the Author

Rachel Hauck is an award winning, *New York Times*, *USA Today*, and *Wall Street Journal* bestselling author.

Her book *The Wedding Dress* was named Inspirational Novel of the Year by *Romantic Times Book Reviews* and has been optioned for film by Brain Power Studio.

She is a double RITA finalist and a Christy and Carol Award Winner.

Her book *Once Upon A Prince*, first in the Royal Wedding Series, was filmed for an Original Hallmark movie.

Rachel was awarded the prestigious Career Achievement Award for her body of original work by *Romantic Times Book Reviews*.

A member of the Executive Board for American Christian Fiction Writers, she teaches workshops and leads worship at the annual conference. She is a past ACFW Mentor of the Year.

At home, she's a wife, writer, worship leader, and works out at a local gym semi-enthusiastically.

A graduate of Ohio State University (Go, Bucks!) with a degree in Journalism, she's a former sorority girl and a devoted Ohio State football fan. Her bucket list is to stand on the sidelines with Ryan Day.

She lives in sunny central Florida with her husband and ornery cat.

For exclusive content and insider information, sign up for her newsletter at www.rachelhauck.com.

Made in the USA
San Bernardino, CA
27 January 2020

63693538R00097